W9-BWA-740

# The Fox Dancer

*Also by Robert J. Steelman*

CHEYENNE VENGEANCE

# The Fox Dancer

## ROBERT J. STEELMAN

DOUBLEDAY & COMPANY, INC.

GARDEN CITY, NEW YORK

1975

All of the characters in this book are fictitious
and any resemblance to actual persons, living or
dead, is purely coincidental.

Library of Congress Cataloging in Publication Data

Steelman, Robert.
The Fox Dancer.

Bibliography: p. 183
I. Title
PZ4.S8145Fo [PS3569.T33847]    813'.5'4
ISBN 0-385-00364-1
Library of Congress Catalog Card Number 74–11818

# The Fox Dancer

# CHAPTER ONE

Now that they had finished their summer pastime of fighting the Crows, they went on the buffalo hunt. The weather was good; it was the Moon When Wolves Run Together. The Oglalas noted with approval the aspens yellow as new-minted gold, the scum of ice on the ponds each morning, the ragged triangular flocks of geese honking in a cloudless sky so blue it hurt the eyes. In no hurry, they paused to gather wild plums and bullberries. Once, where a cavalry patrol had halted long before, they found a volunteer crop of corn where horses on the picket line had scattered grain from their feed. The stalks were higher than a man on a horse, each with three or four large ears still in the milk. That night they lighted a fire and feasted on the succulent corn. They also drank a lot of water. It was their way to insure early rising in anticipation of a long journey.

Next morning a cold mist lay on the land. Like ghosts the twenty Sioux rode in file through the vapors, followed by the packhorses carrying home buffalo meat. Fox Dancer, being the youngest, was in the middle of the line with Lightning Man, his cousin. At the head was Blue Horse, the *wakicunza*, uncle of Fox Dancer and father to Lightning Man. At the rear, alert for anyone trailing them, rode Sun Bull, a scalp-shirt man and leader of the Midnight Strong Hearts Society. Sun Bull was a famous warrior, and insisted on riding at the end of the line in the post of greatest danger.

"I do not see," Lightning Man complained to his cousin, "why they do not let me ride back there sometimes."

Fox Dancer was a quiet and slender young man in his early twenties, and he did not talk much out of deference for his elders. But he was always looking around, watching things, trying to figure out how things came about, what made this do that, why that thing was different from this thing.

"That place is for the bravest man," he explained.

Lightning Man bristled. "What? I am brave too!"

His cousin was three years older; a tall handsome fellow, and very proud. So Fox Dancer only said, "You are brave, all right, cousin. Some day you will take Sun Bull's place."

"You had better say so!" Lightning Man muttered, shaking his lance. "I am as brave as anyone!"

The mists were low, hardly higher than their heads. Watching the line ahead, Fox Dancer occasionally saw a feather-tipped head rise out of the vapors, saw patches of crimson blanket as the fog swirled. In the east a meager glow appeared where the sun tried to pierce the veil. Silently the column moved, the unshod hooves of the ponies making no noise. The air smelled wet and clean; a fragrance of fallen leaves and black forest pools, woodsmoke, horses, rich grass.

Fox Dancer took the carved stick from his war-bag and scratched his head in contentment. Suddenly he paused.

"There!" he whispered, pointing with the stick. "Do you see that, cousin?" A pinprick of light stabbed through the fog and then disappeared.

"What? Where?"

Fox Dancer pointed again. "There! Did you see it? A flash of light!"

Quickly Lightning Man rode to the head of the column, bearer of important news. In a moment the party had gathered in a copse of willows bordering the stream that paralleled their path.

"I saw it too," Blue Horse remarked, loading his Springfield rifle. He was a powerful, broad-chested man with a network of scars from the Sun Dance over his back and shoulders. "A bright light—very bright, then gone."

Sun Bull rode up to join them, a dandy with his government saddle and the mountain-sheep shirt with colored quillwork and decorations of Crow and Pawnee hair, but he was the bravest of them all.

"Buffalo," he said, "do not make bright lights."

Lightning Man started to interrupt, but his father cut him off with a quick gesture. "I think," the *wakicunza* said, "we ought to send two or three men ahead to scout. Then they can come back and tell us what is up there."

As he talked the mist started to lift. Borne by a slight breeze, the vapor drifted away in shreds and tatters. In a matter of seconds the Oglalas sat blinking in the sunlight, feeling the rays warm their chilled bones, but feeling too as if a secret cover had been wrested away. Quickly they shrank into the willows. Fox Dancer, watching his uncle, remembered to pinch together the nostrils of his pony so a whinny could not betray them to whatever lay in the valley beyond.

"There!" Lightning Man cried.

Thigh-deep in the grama grass was a party of the People with Hats, no more than two or three arrow-flights' distant. Some of the white men clustered about a three-legged stand atop which was the shiny object that had winked in the sun. Others were near a wagon, marking on big sheets of paper. On a ragged perimeter were a few blue-clad soldiers. An officer sat a fine-looking big bay and was smoking a pipe.

Forgetting his shyness, Fox Dancer blurted, "What are they doing?"

Blue Horse shrugged his heavy shoulders. "I don't care what they are doing," he said, "They don't belong here. This is Oglala land."

Sun Bull said, "I count ten of them, including the walk-a-heap soldiers."

Lightning Man could not restrain himself any longer. "We have twice as many! And look at that big bay horse! I would like to have that horse! Let's fight them!"

His father coughed in embarrassment. "You talk too much, and too quick," he said.

But Sun Bull rescued him. "If that horse belongs to anyone," the scalp-shirt man growled, "it belongs to me."

In their casual way they sat down in the shade of the willows and wrangled. Blue Horse said, "We are hunting for buffalo.

Our women need meat to pound and dry because it is going to be a cold and hard winter. I think we should pass around these Hat People and look for buffalo."

Sun Bull scooped up a handful of water from the stream and drank long and noisily. Finally he said, "I think we should drive them away. A man needs a good gravy-stirring once in a while." That was what Sun Bull always called a fight; gravy-stirring.

Others were of this opinion and that. Lightning Man, still smarting at the rebuff from his father, joined the discussion. "Some of us," he insisted, "have only bows to hunt with. If we had good guns, like those white men, we would get a lot more buffalo."

Blue Horse turned to Fox Dancer. "What do you think?"

Fox Dancer had been dreaming about the wink of light from the thing atop the three-legged stand. Was it a mirror of some kind? What were they doing with a mirror, these white men, in Oglala country?

"I said, what do you think, nephew?" Blue Horse insisted. "You are always thinking about things. What do you think about it?"

Respectfully Fox Dancer averted his eyes. "Uncle," he said, "I do not think we ought to fight them right now. First, let us see what they are doing. Maybe we can learn something that will help the Oglalas." He made the ritual sign for his people: *cutting off heads*—forefinger extended and drawn sharply across the throat.

"Then—you say?"

"I say wait awhile, and watch."

Lightning Man sniffed. "Do we sit here like old women and wait for them to put their things on the wagons and ride away?" He pointed to the sun, nearly overhead. "Soon night will come. I say fight them, drive them away!"

Sun Bull made a growling noise. "Be quiet," he said. "You are like a magpie, always squawking."

Blue Horse gestured, and they fell silent. The *wakicunza* was a well-known and respected man, even among the Cheyennes and the Crows. He sat for a long time, pondering. When a blue-bodied fly buzzed near and came to rest on his cheek, he still did not move. Finally he opened his eyes and said, "I think we ought to go down and talk to them, tell them they do not belong here, and see what they say."

It was a measure of his stature that no one argued. But the scalp-shirt man looked disappointed; Lightning Man rolled his eyes skyward in a way that said "what can one do with such an old man!"

"You," Blue Horse instructed Sun Bull, "take my son and Fool Dog and go down to them. Tell them they are on Oglala land and they must leave quick or there will be trouble. Do not argue or fight with them. Just speak my words, then come back and tell me what they say."

Sun Bull squatted for a time, leaning on his big Sharps rifle. A little annoyed at the prospect of missing a good fight, he said nothing. Finally he signed his answer. *Maybe they will be angry. Maybe they will try to shoot us.* He held a fist in front of his decorated shirt, snapping fingers rapidly in the *shoot* sign, looking hopeful.

"Not," Blue Horse pointed out, "if you are polite with them and do not argue. We are reasonable. They will be reasonable. Anyway, we are all back here, in the willows, and will come quick if there is trouble."

Sighing, Sun Bull mounted his horse. Lightning Man, pleased at the prospect of excitement, followed him. Fool Dog brought up the rear.

When the white men saw Sun Bull and his two companions, they acted quickly. Those around the shiny instrument ran, abandoning it, and climbed into the wagons, nervously pointing guns. The soldiers, led by the officer on the bay horse, formed a circle around the wagons. When Sun Bull and his companions reined up before the officer, it seemed to Fox Dancer that the whole scene stopped, frozen in brownish tints like the "pick-shers" the photographer at Fort Andrew Jackson had pinned to his wall; the three Oglalas sitting their horses straight and proud before the guns of the white men, fixed bayonets glinting, afternoon sun shedding a flat, hot light over everything, and a cloudless sky beyond.

When the scalp-shirt man raised his arm in greeting, the "picksher" dissolved into life; the spell was broken. The officer's bay horse, nervous, started to dance. There was a small stirring of the white men, a change in the angles of the stiffly poked guns, a waver of action.

"Look at them!" Blue Horse muttered. "They are scared! Scared of three Oglalas!"

When Fox Dancer was a boy, he remembered the *wakicunza* saying that the soldiers at Fort Jackson were good fighters, brave and skillful. But now the white men were having a big war among themselves, back where the sun came each morning. Now, Blue Horse said, the soldiers were mostly cowards and drunkards and troublemakers.

It was quiet in the willows; even the stream seemed to stop its brawling. Motionless, Fox Dancer sat his pony, peering through the screen of leaves. "Be ready," his uncle muttered. "Be ready for anything."

Fox Dancer tightened his grip on the ribboned lance. Firearms were scarce among the Oglalas, reserved for proven warriors like Sun Bull. But in the other hand he clenched the hatchet for which he had given the post trader a bale of prime otter skins.

Down below, the palavering was still going on. Apparently things were not going well. Even from that distance Fox Dancer could hear angry voices, see impatient gestures.

"Things do not look good," Blue Horse whispered. The scars of the Sun Dance stood out pale and taut on his back.

Suddenly Sun Bull twisted in the saddle and pulled aside his scarlet trailing breech-cloth, a foot wide and reaching from his belt to the ground. In a scornful gesture he slapped his bare rump and yelled something to the officer. Angrily the officer kneed the bay forward, pushing it hard against Sun Bull's pony. That was when one of the soldiers, fearful, fired his gun.

"*Hopo!*" Blue Horse shouted. "Let's go!"

Together they dug their heels into their ponies' ribs and sprang from the willows, galloping headlong down the slope, lush with thousands of years of buffalo droppings. As they rode, Sun Bull clutched his chest and fell. Snorting in fear, the pony reared and ran away, dragging Sun Bull by the trailing red sash, which had become entangled in the rigging of his prized saddle. A ragged volley of fire broke out from the wagon, and Fool Dog toppled from his saddle in the act of raising his gun.

"*Hoka hey!*" Blue Horse shouted. It was the ages-old cry of the charge. Behind him others took up the shout. "*Hoka hey! Hoka hey!*" The air rang with whoops, with the pound of hooves on rich, drumlike turf. A curious hawk, drifting low, screamed in alarm and wheeled upward.

"*Hoka hey!*" Fox Dancer shouted. Wind was swift and cool on his cheek. Back there, in the willows, he had sweated. But it was not a sign of fear. Anyone would sweat in that hot, leafy place.

Others, eager for the fight, were trying to pass him. He leaned forward, gathering the pony's ribs with his knees, and the painted horse opened the distance again. It was the first real fight for both of them; for Fox Dancer and for the deer-legged, big-barreled pony, a gift from Blue Horse on the occasion of his nephew's twentieth winter.

In the next instant they were in the fight, a swirling patch-work of bright colors, dust, rearing horses, hatchets flashing in the sun. There were upturned white faces, a hatless officer with hair red as a fox's brush, smell of powder and sweat and blood, screams of fear and anger, churning of men and animals and weapons.

"*Hoka hey!*" Someone was still yelling the charge in Fox Dancer's ear. Then he realized it was himself shouting, shouting, shouting. He swung the hatchet and a soldier staggered back, his face split down the middle like a too-ripe pumpkin.

Suddenly it was over so quickly that they all sat for a moment, exhausted and panting, realizing there were no white men to fight. In the distance a few blue-clad figures plunged into the cover of a grove of willows. The officer, shirt torn off and lacking a boot, had lost his bay horse. He stood at the edge of the trees for a long time, looking at the Oglalas. Then he too disappeared.

In the charge the Oglalas had lost no one. There were a few minor wounds; nothing serious. But Lightning Man was the only survivor of the parley party. Smeared with blood, carrying the head and a piece of the shaft of his broken lance, he was proud and excited. He ran over to a still form and waggled the soldier's stiffly upturned beard.

"*Onhey!*" he shouted. "I killed this one! He shot at me, but it didn't hurt!" Proudly he showed where the ball had torn a furrow in his scalp. "And that one too, over there!" He pointed to a wounded soldier crawling sluglike toward the tall grass. For a moment they all watched the tortured progress. Then the man collapsed and lay still, life running from him like grain from a torn sack.

"What happened?" the *wakicunza* asked. His voice had an edge of anger and bewilderment. "Why did it come about this way?"

"I don't know," Lightning Man said. "Sun Bull pushed the white man's horse with his horse, and told him they were all ugly faces—*ha kin sil yela.* Then someone in the wagon got scared and shot off a gun and Sun Bull fell down and the horse dragged him away." Too excited to restrain himself further, he ran about the battlefield, picking up knives and guns and bandoliers of ammunition.

Blue Horse didn't say anything. Fox Dancer knew his uncle was thinking about Sun Bull and Fool Dog. Someone said, "Let's go after those men that ran away! They don't have horses now. They can't go very far."

The *wakicunza* shook his head. "It will take too long, and it is not worth it. We have given the white men our message, and they will hear about it back at the fort. Right now, that is enough."

The spoils of war were rich; cans of black powder, hundreds of paper cartridges, sacks of lead balls and percussion caps, a lot of food. There were sides of bacon, salt beef, barrels of flour, coffee beans and a mill to grind them, sacks of dried beans and peas. The grass was littered with weapons; Henry repeating rifles, a shotgun with a carved and inlaid stock, Colt and Starr and Remington pistols.

Elated over the haul, the Oglalas did not even bother to pick up their own unbroken and still serviceable arrows. Now they all had guns. No one bothered to strip the clothing from the dead. White men's clothing was ridiculous—heavy and confining. Their boots, especially, were like wooden boxes, stiff and unyielding compared to their own featherlight moccasins.

Excited as children, they caught the wandering horses and improvised pack rigs to transport their booty. Unfortunately the officer's big bay had been wounded in the battle, and someone regretfully cut the horse's throat. They disliked wagons, and although it would slow their progress on the hunt, they needed one to carry their prizes. The harness was queer and unfamiliar; they were accustomed only to their own *travois*. But someone finally figured it out. Only then did they turn to their own slain.

Wrapping Sun Bull and Fool Dog in blankets, they carried them into a grove of cottonwoods. With hatchets they cut branches, lacing them into a rude platform among the fluttering leaves. On the platform they laid the warriors to rest, each with his war-bag, wooden cup, shield, and a supply of pemmican, the good pemmican larded with buffalo tallow and chokecherries, for their sustenance in the next world. At the foot of the tree they stuck two cut saplings into the ground, and to each they tied a dead man's drum, sash, and rattle. Thus they gave the bodies back to the elements, the four winds, the winged things of the air.

Waving the rest of them on, Blue Horse stood for a long time at the foot of the cottonwood, looking at the fluttering sashes, listening to the rattles as they rasped dryly in the wind. Fox Dancer knew his uncle was thinking about the fight. Blue Horse was thinking maybe he should have listened to the others and attacked the white men without warning. In that way, maybe Sun Bull and Fool Dog would be riding away with them. That was, Fox Dancer suddenly realized, what made his uncle a great leader. Always, after a decision, Blue Horse wondered if he had acted wisely.

Carrying the shiny three-legged machine that was his prize from the battle of the willows, Fox Dancer stopped at the summit of the ridge, looking back. His uncle had mounted his pony and rode slowly toward them. It was late; the sun was tilting down the long slope toward the west, and the night would be cold. This had been an important day for Fox Dancer; important in some way he only felt, and did not understand.

⟷

The hunting to the east was not good. The Oglalas found only scattered buffalo, and those few were frightened and wary. The plain was littered with carcasses from which the hides had been stripped; white men had been there, also. Reluctantly, they decided to turn back toward the Black Hills. Even if the hunting was bad, they had captured a lot of food in the battle; perhaps on the way back they could pick up a few straggling bulls against the winter. So they dawdled on the trail, took their time, enjoyed the rays of the slowly failing sun. Winter would soon be on the land; this was their last outing of the year.

After the exultation of the big gravy-stirring, they now felt dispirited. Certain things happened that made them suspect that the gods were angry. First, of course, was the bad hunting. Then, things kept mysteriously disappearing from camp. Bad luck dogged them. One member of the party cut his foot while chopping wood, and the wound grew ugly and inflamed, dripping a yellow discharge. Unseasonably, it rained; for three days they moved listless and wet through the downpour, and some of the precious flour was spoiled.

A *sikisn*, a ghost, seemed to be following them. Perhaps the *sikisn* was the spirit of one of the dead soldiers. Maybe, the Oglalas thought, they had somehow offended Rock, their patron god of war. Maybe even *Wakan Tanka*, the Great One Above, did not like them anymore.

For example, Little Man rolled out of his blanket one frost-sharp morning to find his new fifteen-shot Henry rifle missing. They searched everywhere for it, but didn't find it. Some thought it might have dropped from Little Man's saddle on the trail, but he angrily denied it. He had, he insisted, put it beside him before he slept.

Again, one night Goosey had a strong dream about a bear, a giant bear which was chasing him. He woke up yelling; the dream seemed so real he grabbed his lance and went prowling around the sodden camp, jabbing bushes with it. And indeed, while they were all poking fun at Goosey, often a butt for their jokes because of his touchy loins, some large animal crashed away into the brush. They ran after it but never found anything. Well, it had all been a dream. But what did it mean?

The odd happenings continued. Twigs cracked when no one was near, food disappeared. The Oglalas, now uneasy, wove charms from magpie feathers and sacred grasses, chanted prayers, even threw into the fire some prized coffee beans to propitiate the gods. But nothing worked.

Blue Horse tried to reassure them. "It happens this way sometimes," he explained. "A person does not have a good heart, and the gods send down a *sikisn* to follow in his steps and cause trouble."

But who was the person with the bad heart?

Blue Horse was still worried about his decision to send Sun Bull to parley with the white men. "Maybe," he admitted, "I am the person with the bad heart. Maybe Rock is angry with me." So he made a sweat lodge from bent saplings with his blanket thrown over them and stayed in the steam for several hours, emerging purified, so he told them. But when they woke the next morning, the *sikisn* had struck a deadly blow. One Horn, a cousin of Sun Bull, was missing. The grass appeared crushed and trampled where he had been dragged away. During the night no one had heard anything, yet the man had vanished.

Fearful and hesitant, they followed the all-too-plain trail. The body, throat cut, lay at the edge of a stream, half hidden in a thicket of bullberries. The moccasins and shirt were gone, and the bare, dead feet waggled in the current as the water foamed over them.

Afraid the *sikisn* might still be near, the Oglalas buried One Horn where they had found him, then moved on. That night the mood of the camp was one of black despair. What had they done wrong? Fox Dancer was the youngest, and so kept silent when the older men discussed the matter. Kills Often was speaking.

"I am not going to eat meat anymore," he said, tossing a gnawed bone into the fire. "After tonight, I take no meat. Everyone knows when a man does not eat meat, his dreams get better. I want to have a good strong dream that will tell us what to do."

Broken Dish did not think much of the idea. "What we need," he objected, "is the root of a red-flowered plant I know about. I will find some tomorrow. When you chew up the root and smear it on your forehead and your chest and your belly, then no *sikisn* can harm you."

Others had different suggestions. Goosey swore never to touch iron again; no kettle, no knife, nothing made of iron. It was iron, he said, that attracted bad spirits. Someone else had an extra wife he would give away when they got back to the Black Hills, in order to show he was generous and great-spirited. Rock would look down and see this, and call off the *sikisn*. Then Lightning Man entered rudely into the discussion.

"I know what the trouble is," he blurted.

They all looked at him, astonished.

Pointing to the shiny brass instrument on its tripod, he went on, "That is what the trouble is all about."

Fox Dancer moved instinctively to protect the instrument. "What are you talking about?" he demanded.

"I mean that thing there," Lightning Man shouted, a little embarrassed at his own rashness but going ahead anyhow. "That thing is some kind of a god to the white man. Look how it stands on three legs and winks at us in the light from the fire! Fox Dancer took one of the white man's gods, and it is causing bad luck."

"Foolishness," Fox Dancer laughed. "Foolishness!"

But some began to stir anxiously and whisper among themselves. Even Blue Horse looked concerned, saying, "Maybe

Lightning Man is right. He talks too much and says foolish things, but a chattering squirrel can warn of danger."

Bolder, Lightning Man got to his feet and swaggered toward the instrument. "Look at it!" he insisted. "Just look at it! Round things are good things, we all know that. The sun is round, the moon is round, Oglala lodges are round, we always camp in a circle; everything good is round. But this evil thing! It is sharp and shiny and made up of a lot of straight sticks and bones and things. It is bad, I say—very bad! As long as we carry it with us, we are going to have bad luck!"

When his cousin raised the hatchet as if to harm the instrument, Fox Dancer kicked out, catching the inside of Lightning Man's thigh and hooking his own toe so that the youth sprawled flat. "Don't speak any more foolish words," Fox Dancer warned.

His cousin was shamed before the elders. He sprang to his feet; with his free hand he made the classic sign of contempt— thumb poked obscenely between the two middle fingers: *eat excrement.* Crouched slightly, poising the hatchet, he circled Fox Dancer, making the prescribed brave grunts, like the bear, to show he was ready for a fight.

"I do not fight you," Fox Dancer insisted. "There should be no fight between us, cousin." Turning as Lightning Man circled, he kept between the youth and the instrument on its tripod. "We are friends."

But Lightning Man was furious. "Take out your knife!" he called. "There has to be blood to wash out what is between us!"

Watching his cousin's every catlike movement, Fox Dancer still did not draw his knife. Someone at the edge of the circle of firelight moved as if to break up the fight, but Blue Horse raised his hand. This was between Fox Dancer and Lightning Man. Perhaps it was the best way to settle a disagreement that might imperil the whole party. Besides, in this way Rock might speak to them, advise them.

Suddenly rushing, Lightning Man swung the hatchet. Fox Dancer ducked under it, catching Lightning Man in the belly with a hard-driven shoulder. But Lightning Man fell across him, and under the weight of his cousin's body Fox Dancer fell to the ground. Together the two rolled about, clawing, scratching, biting. They hurtled into the fire, scattering flaming brands. Fox Dancer smelled smoke and scorched flesh, blood from his forearm where Lightning Man had bitten to the bone.

"A fool, am I?" his cousin snarled in his ear as they rolled into the high grass. "Speak foolishness, do I?"

Lightning Man had his fingers locked about Fox Dancer's throat. Try as he would, Fox Dancer could not break that iron-fingered grip. His cousin was only three years older, but always had been taller and heavier.

Flattened, Lightning Man bending over him and pressing his full weight down onto the locked fingers, Fox Dancer felt his head swim, his vision fail, the pulse in his ears loud and heavy and threatening. Maybe the shiny instrument was indeed an evil god; perhaps he had been wrong to take it. Now it was having its revenge; the gods of the white men were powerful, too.

In a last, desperate fit of effort he kicked upward with his knee, catching Lightning Man in the groin. It was effective. With a sudden gasp his cousin slackened the grip. Clutching his genitals, he toppled over and lay in the grass, moaning.

Fox Dancer swayed to his feet and staggered away to lean against the trunk of a gnarled juniper that poked from a rocky ledge. His mouth was full of blood from battered lips and broken teeth; his lungs could not draw in enough air to sustain him; his body trembled like an aspen leaf in the wind. Then— his moccasined foot touched something soft in the grass beneath the juniper. In fright he drew back, blinking, trying to see into the darkness of the grass. A snake? A small animal? What?

That was how they caught the *sikisn.*

# CHAPTER TWO

The ghost sprang up and ran, slipping and clattering in loose shale. Fox Dancer could only lean dazedly against the juniper, rubbing his throat, watching the Oglalas pursue the *sikisn* till they trapped it in a rocky cleft. There was a great deal of shouting and confusion, and two or three shots. But finally they caught the ghost, bound its hands, and brought it down the littered slope and into camp. Someone tossed dry wood on the scattered embers, and flames leaped up.

It was the red-headed officer from the battle of the willows. Clad in stolen moccasins and stolen shirt, he stood stony-eyed and defiant before them, a small, compact man whose green-blue eyes glittered in the firelight. He had been carrying Little Man's fifteen-shot Henry rifle, and a beaded war-bag over his shoulder was stuffed with Oglala meat and corn and dried berries. In spite of his privations, the officer looked tough and sinewy, and glared menacingly at them.

"*Sha, sha!*" Blue Horse chuckled. "Good, very good!" He walked up to the prisoner and looked carefully at him. "So this is our *sikisn*. This is the bad luck that followed us all the way."

Excited and laughing, the Oglalas crowded around the white man, poking at him, stroking the silky red hair and beard. The officer was contemptuous, only staring straight ahead, saying nothing.

Lightning Man had forgotten the quarrel. Unsheathing his knife, he pricked the white skin that showed under the edge of the officer's stolen shirt. The prisoner winced, but did not cry out.

"I want his hair!" Broken Dish cried. He grabbed a handful

of it, twisting the man's head askew, and waved his knife. "Did you ever see such hair? It is good luck, that hair. No one has hair like that hanging on his shirt!"

The pelt was indeed impressive; long, silky, catching the flames in little highlights. It shone rich and russet, like the brush of a fox at the end of summer when it has had its fill of young mice and rabbits.

"It belongs to me!" someone else insisted. "I grabbed away his rifle before he could shoot anybody!" Others put in their claims. "Fox Dancer and I were fighting," Lightning Man insisted. "If we hadn't been fighting and come near to where that soldier was lying in the grass, no one would have found him!" He even appealed to Fox Dancer for justice. "Isn't that right? Speak, cousin!"

Blue Horse had had enough of the quarreling. Seizing a lance, he flailed about with the shaft, driving them away like camp dogs. It was a dishonor for anyone to be struck with a stick, and they scattered.

"Leave him alone!" the *wakicunza* shouted. "I will decide what to do!"

Still there was dissension. Someone said, "We ought to kill him right now. White men bring trouble." Another said, "Sun Bull and Fool Dog are dead. I saw this one shoot Sun Bull when he was only trying to talk sense to them." Lightning Man, still eyeing the richness of the captive's hair, started to sidle around in back of the prisoner.

In fact, it was only reasonable to kill the white man. But Fox Dancer interrupted.

"Wait!" His voice was husky and reedlike, and it hurt him to speak. "Wait," he said again, spitting out some blood and a tooth.

They waited. Finally he asked, "Does a man kill a good pony when it kicks him? Does a man refuse to eat a fat dog because dogs bark sometimes, and cause trouble?"

Though relieved that the tension had been broken, Blue Horse looked puzzled. "I don't know what you mean," he finally said.

"This man," Fox Dancer explained, "must be a chief of the walk-a-lots. Look at the gold things on his shoulders! He wears One Horn's shirt, but he has pinned his gold things to it. And he rode a fine horse at The Battle of the Willows. It is plain the white people are fond of him, and he is important. We should keep him, take him with us to our camp. When we need some things—flour, coffee, bullets, tobacco—then we can trade the white man for them."

There was silence, doubtful silence. Then Blue Horse spoke.

"Yes. I think you are right. You always think things out in your head. If we kill him, what have we got? Nothing. But if we keep him, he is as good in trade as horses or bales of furs or anything else."

The white man looked steadily at Fox Dancer. Did the prisoner speak Sioux? Did he understand what they were talking about? Fox Dancer knew some English from trading at Fort Jackson. He was always quick to pick up languages and signs. "Understand?" he said in English to the white man.

The man did not reply. But Fox Dancer felt a quickening of his senses. Something passed between him and the fox-haired officer. After all, he himself was Fox Dancer. This sullen prisoner was of the foxes, too. With that rich pelt, there could be no doubt.

Finally they agreed. They would take the white man back to the Black Hills, and his disposition would be decided there. They agreed, that is, except for Lightning Man and a few others. Suddenly Lightning Man remembered their quarrel. Muttering, he glowered at Fox Dancer. Fox Dancer only turned away, but not before hearing his cousin's warning:

"This white man will cause us all a lot of trouble. And it is your fault, cousin!"

↔

It was hard for Lew Duffy to decide whether he was more furious at being captured, or frightened at being spared. As a soldier, his rashness had gotten him into trouble. As a soldier, he was prepared to die for his rashness. But as a man, he trembled at the prospect that the Oglalas were saving him for elegant torture. Hands bound behind his back, feet tied under the horse's belly, he muttered a string of Hail Marys. Good soldier, bad Catholic; that had been the story of his life.

It began to snow—a misty downpour through which the sun perversely glowed. Behind Duffy rode the scowling young brave who had been in the scuffle last night. From time to time the youth rode up to him, jerking roughly at his bonds to make sure they were tight. That one, Duffy thought, would like to have my hair. The other one, the younger, with the impassive face, threw a tattered blanket over Lew's shoulders against the cold. Duffy was, for the moment at least, to be preserved.

The war party was going west. Duffy tried to make out some of their conversation, but without success. Captain Logan at the post was fluent in Sioux, and was in fact compiling a Sioux dictionary for the brass back at the War Department. From John Logan, Duffy had picked up a lot of words and signs, but right now the Oglala talk seemed mostly grunts and murmurs.

Of course, he should have put out pickets to warn of the approach of danger. But it had been a peaceful October afternoon with no sign of Sioux when Duffy and his command had left Fort Jackson with the railroad-route surveyors. Now the devils had butchered the work party, decimated his command, set him afoot. Sweet Jesus, how was *that* going to look on his record! But the two B Company privates who'd fled the field with him had finally deserted, terror-struck by his plan to follow the Oglalas and fight them. So Duffy had tracked the savages on foot, stolen a rifle and ammunition and moccasins and food. By God, given a little time and luck he would have destroyed them all! But he had had no horse, and while the Oglalas seemed to dawdle along, taking the sun and smoking their pipes often, it was all he could do to keep up with them, afoot as he was. Duffy had to have a mount to keep up with them. And that was how he had come to be caught.

The Oglala ponies were grazing near a rocky ledge, and he wriggled near a pinto, murmuring soothingly. But the brute suddenly wandered to a more succulent patch of grass at the edge of the circle of firelight where the Sioux sat palavering. Mildly curious, the beast gazed at him for a while, then went back to wrenching up grass.

After losing his boot in the fight, his foot was damnably sore and festered. Foolishly, perhaps, he wriggled closer. The dangling nose-rope was almost in his grasp. Then the fight erupted among the warriors. Nervous, the pony pranced away, leaving Duffy hiding in the tall grass.

For some time he had been aware of rising voices, angry gestures, argument among the braves. But how could he suspect that the fight would surge up the slope toward him; that the one warrior, the one who kicked the other in the crotch, would— *sweet Jesus*—step on Duffy himself!

For two days they bore westward. The weather grew steadily colder, the sun disappeared, the skies grew leaden-gray. A bitter wind whirled across the plain. The Oglalas rode in silence, paying no more attention to their prisoner than the plunder they were transporting in the stolen wagon: the flour, bacon, beef, black powder, and the rest. Lew Duffy was only one more commodity. The scowling young man once struck Duffy across the face when he found the prisoner's wrist bonds loosened. But the elder who seemed to be running the party reproved the youth; there were no more incidents.

In an unseasonable snowstorm they crossed several creeks, horses slipping and falling as hooves broke though thin ice. Trying to remember his maps, and the lay of the land, Duffy thought one of them must surely be the south fork of Horse Creek. In that case Fort Jackson could be no more than forty miles to the north. But in weather like this no cavalry patrols were out. Anyway, the savages kept resolutely to their westward course, winding through snow-topped buffalo grass and sagebrush toward the ramparts of the Black Hills.

Somewhere in the foothills the column filed up a shale-littered canyon, bluffs on either side bare and somber outcroppings of yellow clay, slate, and sandstone. The bitter wind was broken and Duffy felt somewhat warmer. He did not have a thermometer, but estimated the reading at thirty degrees or so on the

Fahrenheit scale. In spite of his discomfort he kept a careful watch of his surroundings. If he lived, he might someday have the opportunity to come back to this country and wipe out the red bastards.

The path grew steeper and more rocky, and ponies floundered in drifted snow. From time to time some of the braves dismounted and cut cottonwood poles with which they wedged and prized the wagon wheels through the boulder-littered bed of the canyon. Now snow fell so heavily it was impossible to see more than a dozen yards ahead. Oddly enough, the party seemed to grow more cheerful. There were jokes, laughter, almost a holiday mood.

There was a reason. In another half mile or so, the canyon debouched into a broad, grassy bowl, hemmed about with stands of pine and juniper. Across the snowy plain Duffy saw a large Sioux village, dozens of lodges, glowing in the twilight like giant lighted tapers. Through falling snow people came running to greet the party. Dogs barked, children screamed with excitement, youths clambered into the wagon to drag out weapons, sacks of grain, cans of black powder, barrels of salt beef. Around the wagon the elders clamored, marveling at the riches. A young girl, dark braids bound in otter fur, came up to Lew and touched him, smiling, then ran away.

After a while someone cut the thongs that bound Duffy's wrists and ankles. Half frozen, feet and hands like roughly carved blocks of wood, he stood knee-deep in fresh snow, wondering what was to happen. But they only led him away to one of the glowing *tipis*, holding the flap and gesturing him to enter.

It was too dark and smoky to take note of the furnishings of his new home. There were Oglalas there, sitting on piled furs, and Duffy could smell meat cooking. But he had hardly slept for days, and it was warm in the lodge. He stumbled toward the buffalo robe near the fire and collapsed.

Sometime during the night he woke. The other occupants of the lodge slept soundly. Wincing with pain, he crept to the doorflap and looked out.

The Oglala camp lay silent in the moonlight. From a distant

peak a wolf howled, and there was an answering chorus of yips from the dense woods. It had stopped snowing; the moon shone so brightly on fields of white it hurt his eyes. Their ponies moved palely in a brush corral at the edge of the trees. For a moment a thought stirred at the edge of his mind. Escape?

Then reality settled heavily on him. Of course no one was watching him. Of course the ponies were not guarded. The Oglala camp slept soundly, peacefully, with no care nor worry. Soldiers could not ascend that rocky, boulder-strewn canyon, choked with drifts that by now must be over a man's head. And —no soldier could get out, either.

Tottering back into the lodge, he pulled the buffalo robe about him. He wanted to fight someone, but there was no one, nothing, to fight. After a while he began to weep, not from fear but from frustration. He pounded a clenched fist into the smoky-smelling fur of the robe. No one paid attention. The Oglalas only slept. After a while, spent and bitter, Lew Duffy slept also.

↔

Two old people lived in the lodge; a wrinkle-faced elder with dwarfed and twisted legs, and his wife. In the morning the woman brought Duffy meat stew and a tin cup of coffee. He wolfed the stew and sipped gratefully at the steaming coffee. Afterward, he held out the cup in a mute gesture.

"*Pazuta sapa*," the old woman said, smiling. She poured more, smacking her lips. "*Pazuta sapa.*"

Maybe that was the word for coffee. *Pazuta sapa.* He thanked her moodily. God, how he wished he had his pipe and some Lone Jack! But he had lost his pipe in the fight, and the Oglalas had taken his tobacco.

Dragging withered legs, the old man came crablike to sit beside him, staring in a not unfriendly manner. Finally he touched the stubble on Duffy's chin. "*Sha!*" he chuckled.

*Sha*, indeed! Red. Duffy remembered that word. Yes, the red beard of Irish kings. *Sha* was red; *sha sha* meant good. By signs he made the woman know he wanted a mirror. She brought him one, a broken fragment with the back peeling, but apparently precious.

Sweet Jesus! A wild man stared back at him; hair matted and dirty, once-neatly-trimmed beard now brushy and disheveled. His eyes were sunk in reddened rims, nose pinched and weeping from the cold.

Well, Lew Duffy was still a soldier. He would have to police himself a little. Perceiving what he wanted, the old man rummaged in a buffalo-hide trunk rich with painted suns and moons, and found a rusty, white man's razor. With the razor, and cold water made soapy with a root the woman shredded into it, Duffy hacked away. After a while his chin was bloody, but smooth. He combed his hair with his fingers, wrapped the ragged blanket about his shoulders, and stepped into the morning sun.

During his short tour at Fort Jackson, Lew Duffy had seen many Sioux. They were uniformly poor specimens, despised as "cracker and molasses" Indians. The Platte Road was plagued with them; ragged, lice-infested men, women, and children whining around emigrant wagons, trying to cadge tobacco, bread, bacon, anything. Once a month the government agent gave them a few beeves, and passed out flour and coffee. But long before the next slaughtering time the Indians ran out of food. *Wagluhke*, John Logan called these Indians. Beggars. The real hard-cases, the ones Lew Duffy had gone west to fight, rarely came to the post except to trade furs for powder and ball, tobacco, or coffee. The hard-cases, Logan said, despised the *wagluhke* too, calling them "hang-around-the-fort people."

But this was no village of beggars! Dogs barked, children shrieked with laughter as they rode buffalo-rib sleds on the new snow. In a sunwarmed corner, protected from the wind by a screen of hides, an old man cut up a tin frying pan with a chisel so as to make arrowheads. At the edge of the trees young boys were chopping cottonwood branches to feed the horses. A bevy of girls carrying water buckets made of hide slipped past Duffy, giggling and shy, and ran toward the frozen stream. "If I had half a chance," Duffy muttered, "I know what I'd do to you, my girls!" Curls of smoke spiraled upward from lodges, and beside each *tipi* a rack of poles held dried meat, now dusted with snow. Against the cold the men of the village wore buffalo-skin moccasins with high tops, and leggings of blue woolen cloth. Many had elaborate buckskin shirts with the hair outside. Almost all, including the women, had red trade blankets over their shoulders. They were warmly and comfortably dressed, and moved about with pride and intent.

Fascinated, Duffy wandered through the village. No one moved to stop him. Someday he and the Eighth would come back to this Oglala village; against that day he stored important tactical data in his head. The notch in the hills to the north might mean an alternate entrance to the village. A cannon, if they could get one in, would sweep the whole village from the slope where the children were sledding.

But people stared at him, some tittered. It made him furious. After all, these were hostiles! These were people who had slaughtered the railroad surveyors, run off Lieutenant Duffy's detachment of soldiers, taken Duffy himself prisoner, and humiliated him!

He could stand anything but to be taken lightly. Once, long ago in Dublin, he had shot a man for taking him lightly. It had been in a pub, and Duffy had to leave Trinity College and run. That was one reason he was in America; it was one reason he was now strolling about an Oglala village and being snickered at.

Red-faced and angry, he went back to the *tipi* and sat for a long time, glowering at the dying coals of the fire. Neither the crippled man nor the woman approached him. Perhaps they were frightened.

↔

The next morning they brought him into a big council lodge that sat apart from the others. Blue Horse, as camp leader or *wakicunza*, was there, along with other members of the war party; Broken Dish, Fox Dancer, Kills Often, Lightning Man, Goosey, and others. But Blue Horse did not preside. As *wakicunza*, he was concerned principally with camp administration; instead, Elk River, senior of the scalp-shirt men, or hereditary chiefs, sat on the wolf skin at the center of the circle, facing the doorflap, with Bear Tooth, the shaman, at his side.

"So this is the crazy white man," Elk River said to Blue Horse. "The *sikisn.*"

"Yes."

"He looks like a fox. See the bright hair, the long nose, the sharp eyes."

Blue Horse agreed.

"His skin is white, very white," the scalp-shirt chief mused. "More white than I have ever seen. Is he frightened? Is that why he has turned so white?"

Blue Horse took the proffered pipe, blowing ceremonial rings to each of the four directions, with a courteous added puff overhead to the Great One Above, *Wakan Tanka.*

"Maybe. But he can bite, that fox. He is brave!"

Elk River got up and walked close to the prisoner. Others crowded around, poking at the red-haired man, feeling his skin, pulling his hair. The officer only stared straight ahead with his blue-green eyes. Someone pinched him hard and hopefully, but the white man did not flinch.

Elk River went back to sit on the wolf skin, and smoked for a long time. Finally he said to Blue Horse, "What shall we do with him?"

Blue Horse indicated his son. "Lightning Man says the white man is bad luck. We should kill him right now. But"—he nodded toward Fox Dancer—"he thinks we should keep him, trade him at Fort Jackson for flour or black powder or what we need."

There was much opinion from the rest of the council; some supported Lightning Man, some Fox Dancer. But Elk River raised his ceremonial painted stick with the eagle feather topping it, and the clamor stilled.

"Let us think about this man," Elk River said.

He sat for a long time, smoking. The lodge, warmed by the council fire, became hot. Blue smoke twisted upward in a slanting shaft of sun that entered through the smoke flap. The lodge smelled of bodies, tobacco, paint, woodsmoke, the buffalo fat they mixed with ocher and vermilion to paint their faces and bodies. Little by little the white man began to sweat. Glasslike beads formed on his long nose and dripped, the narrow face grew even paler, but still the prisoner stared stonily at Elk River and did not tremble. Lightning Man sidled near the prisoner and made a gesture. It was the motion of drawing a bow and releasing the arrow. "Tcchk!" he hissed. It was such a remarkable imitation of the speeding of an arrow that several of them shouted "*Hau! Hau!*" laughing and applauding. But the prisoner still did not flinch.

Finally Elk River spoke.

"We have talked to a lot of them at Fort Jackson," he said, "and we have killed some. We ought to know more about them. Fox Dancer is right. He is young, but"—Elk River jabbed out his thumb in the sign for *truth*—"he speaks sense."

Lightning Man, lingering near the prisoner, started to protest. His father cut him off with a sharp gesture.

"Fox Dancer speaks sense," Elk River repeated. "Maybe it is a good idea to keep this white man here, with us. We ought to study him like we study the deer and the buffalo and the rest of the animals that are the children of *Wakan Tanka*. In that way we will learn much, and know how to deal with the white man."

It was a statesmanlike decision. Most agreed, shouting, "*Hau, hau!*" But there were a few dissenters. Lightning Man flung out a question.

"How do we know he will not run away, bring the walk-a-heaps to our camp? That is something to think about."

Bear Tooth, the doctor, soothsayer, and prophet of the camp, jumped up, roach of porcupine hair waggling with indignation. "What do you know about what will happen?" he demanded. "You are a child, and talk foolishness!" The shaman touched the stuffed yellowhammer that hung from a thong around his neck. "This bird is a sacred bird. He tells me what *Wakan Tanka* wants." Cocking his head as if listening to bird talk, Bear Tooth closed his eyes. The rest fell respectfully silent, though Lightning Man still glowered and muttered.

Finally Bear Tooth opened his eyes. He waved his feathered rattle in Lightning Man's face. "The white man should be kept here for a while. That is what *Wakan Tanka* says."

After the Great One Above had spoken, there could be no
further argument. Someone lifted the flap, and sun streamed
in. They all went out laughing and joking, while the white man
shambled back to the lodge of Man-Who-Never-Walked and his
wife, Twin Woman. Only Fox Dancer and Lightning Man remained in the council lodge, eyeing each other.

"Cousin," Fox Dancer said, "maybe you are right, maybe I
am right. No one knows. Someday we will find out." He held out
his palm. "Touch my hand, friend."

Lightning Man looked this way and that, not wanting to meet
Fox Dancer's eyes. Finally he slapped out a hand in a grudging
gesture that met his cousin's fingers only in passing.

"We are friends, all right," he conceded. "I guess we are
friends. Your father and my father were brothers. There is blood
in us from them both. Your father was a good man. He had
goodwill to all the people, and kept an even temper and never
was stingy with food. He gave away a lot of his horses, and his
name was great. But I think you are wrong, cousin. Sometimes if
I get very angry it is because I think you do not know what you
are doing, and bring trouble on the Oglalas."

With a moccasined toe Fox Dancer kicked dirt over the smoldering council fire.

"We will see," he said. "Sometimes danger has to be risked to
bring down the bear."

↔

After the first hard snowfall of the season, there was a brief
respite. Streams thawed, birds sang, spots of color appeared on
the hillsides where flowers were deceived by the warmth into
unseasonable bloom. In their casual way the Oglalas went about
the business of preparing for winter. The women put away in
leather boxes the corn, beans, and squash they had traded from
the Rees and dried in the sun. They gathered chokecherries and
wild plums, pounded pemmican, ground sage leaves for an oint-
ment against frostbite, melted buffalo tallow around cloth wicks
to serve as candles. In the failing sun the women sat murmuring
woman-talk to each other while they scraped hides and sewed

dyed porcupine quills and trade beads onto winter shirts for their men.

They were too busy to pay any attention to the white man wandering free about the camp. The red-headed officer was a brave man, and in spite of his peculiar ways they respected him. Besides, he was good to the children, and sang to them and made jokes. Too, Bear Tooth consulted his yellowhammer and told them all that the first great blizzard of winter was coming, if not this day, then the next; no more than a week at most. Taking advantage of the sun, the Oglalas worked against the winter and paid no attention to Duffy.

Just before the blizzard struck, the red-haired man stole a pony and fled through the high pass to the north of the Oglala camp. Most of the people thought it was all right, though they were of several minds as to his motivation. After all, even a foolish white man does not flee into the wilderness in the face of a blizzard. Perhaps Duffy was frightened of Lightning Man, who still wanted the officer's hair. Perhaps Duffy wanted to die. Or perhaps—this was very likely—the red-headed man was just foolish and headstrong, and thought he could reach Fort Jackson.

Anyway, *Wakan Tanka* had spoken. This was the Great One's way of settling the question. After all, who could travel more than a few miles in that swirling snow, wind raking like the claws of a hungry bear?

But Fox Dancer took his favorite horse and some provisions and went after the white man. After a long search, with the officer's tracks quickly obliterated by the snow, he found Lew Duffy in a snowdrift ten or fifteen miles from the Oglala camp. Duffy was frozen and blue in appearance, hair and beard laced with ice. The stolen pony had broken a leg on an icy ledge, and Duffy had slit its throat with a stolen knife. The puddles of blood, frozen into icy disks, shone like gold in the winter sun that now emerged from the racks of scudding cloud.

It took two days of hard work, but Fox Dancer finally got Duffy back to the camp. His own hands and feet were badly frostbitten in the process, but Duffy lived. Fox Dancer had had a dream, and bringing Duffy back from death was part of it.

# CHAPTER THREE

The Oglalas, like all the Sioux, had their Winter Calendar—a long, historical record of The People. Each winter was identified by a particular event. There was The Winter When The Mandan Houses Were Burned, The Winter When The People Fought On The Ice, The Winter When High Hump Was Killed. There were no written records; the litany was contained in the heads of shamans like Bear Tooth, passed down by rote from father to son. Some of the winters dated a hundred years back, like The Swimming For Buffalo Winter. Some dealt with historic and important events, like The Winter The People First Saw Steel Knives. Others remembered disease and sickness, such as The Winter Of The Smallpox. Still others referred to more trivial events, like The Winter When Penis Was A Log. There was at that time an Oglala man named Penis, a bad person whom nobody liked. When they were all playing a game which involved rolling a log down a slope, Penis got very mad at someone and struck him. The man killed Penis, and they went on playing the roll-the-log game, using Penis's body instead of a log.

This winter was to go down as The Winter When The Trees Made A Noise. The weather was cold, streams froze thick, there was snow to the depth of a pony's withers. The trees, too, froze solid. In the middle of the night it was not unusual to hear a sound like a pistol shot as a pine tree split from the pressure of ice crystals forming within it.

Lew Duffy's eyes had been injured—from freezing, or perhaps it was snow-blindness—and two of the women rubbed gunpowder into them according to their practice. After lying for several days half dead in the lodge of Man-Who-Never-Walked,

not knowing whether he was dreaming or already at the portals
of heaven, the searing pain of the gunpowder brought Duffy
back to full consciousness. Screaming and struggling, he tried to
get away from the two females. They held him down, speaking
gently, and after a while the pain subsided.

It was three days before he could see clearly. Then he made
out dim figures moving in the lodge, and after a while faces, out-
lines, even some details.

"What's your name?" he muttered to the Indian girl bending
over him, feeding him broth with a horn spoon.

She spoke no English, but there was something in his face that
told her what he wanted to know. She obviously liked pretty
shells, and had a necklace of them about her throat, others
sewed to her dress. "*Cha na,*" she murmured.

He looked at her for a long time, the smooth brow, dark
braids wrapped in otter fur, the concern in her eyes. Why, this
was the girl who had come laughing up to him when they
brought him to the Oglala camp—the one who had dared to
touch him, then ran away! But there was none of that tomboy-
ishness about her now; she was a woman.

"*Chana,*" Duffy repeated. That meant *shell*, he remembered
from John Logan's dictionary.

The girl shook her head. "*Cha na.*" Two separate vowels.

Hearing them, Twin Woman bustled over, bringing a cup of
water poured from a hide bag. Ugly as a basket of warts, that
old woman was, but she was kind, too. It unsettled Duffy to have
savages kind to him. Why in hell hadn't they let him die in the
snow? He had been disgraced anyway—lost his command, foolishly pursued the Oglalas, been captured because of his rashness,
now unaccountably saved from a winter death by these savages.
Angrily he pushed away the water.

"Don't want it," he muttered, and slept again.

The big *tipi* was surprisingly warm and comfortable. Drowsing
in his buffalo robe, he wondered how they did it. There must be
a kind of underground air intake, and it brought outside air into
the base of the always-burning fire. There it was warmed, and
eventually went upward and out the smoke flap. From the shad-

ows on the hide walls, Duffy judged also that snow was banked high around the outside of the *tipi*, and that helped, too. In their own way these people certainly knew how to deal with winter. But they had taken his clothes and left him naked! He complained long and loud, but was too weak to do anything else. The old, crippled man dragged himself over and watched him for a long time, but that didn't do Duffy any good. Emotion left him sweating and upset. When the girl *Cha na* came in again, brushing snow from her braids, he pulled the robe over his head, embarrassed, refusing the horn spoon and the more substantial stew they were now giving him. Goddamnit, he was naked— mother naked!

Hidden under the robe, he did, however, listen with pleasure to her soft entreaties. Sioux talk had seemed to Duffy for the most part a harsh, choking, sibilant noise. But he had heard only men speak it. *Cha na's* Sioux seemed musical, liquid, filled with soft diphthongs, almost like Gaelic. If he only had his clothes he would like to sit up and look at her.

Someone else came to the lodge, too; the impassive young brave who had been in the squabble the night Duffy was caught. Slight for an Oglala, he squatted beside Duffy and stared, saying nothing. Duffy fidgeted. His visitor was apparently an important person, because the old woman and the crippled man moved humbly away into a corner of the lodge. The girl called Shell went back to boiling meat in a hide-lined pit with heated rocks taken from the fire.

"Well," Duffy complained, "what the hell?"

The young man continued to stare at him, face somber.

"I mean," Duffy said, "what the hell are you staring at?"

The visitor knew some English. Still unsmiling, he said, "Me —name—" Here he murmured something in Sioux, which Duffy didn't understand. Then he went on. "Fox Dancer. Me." He tapped his beaded chest. "English name Fox Dancer."

"Look here," Duffy protested, "I want my pants. You savvy— pants." He pulled aside the robe to explain. "Goddamnit, they took all my clothes!"

The young man, Fox Dancer, spoke to the girl. She said something, then giggled. When Fox Dancer turned back, his face was somber but there was a glint of mirth in his eyes.

"You clothes," he said. "You clothes all"—he searched for a word, and made a quick gesture, pointing to the ground and then rubbing the tips of his fingers together—"dirty. You clothes dirty. She throw away."

Duffy howled in frustration. "What in hell am I going to wear?"

Later, when he was able to walk a little, they gave him Sioux clothing; a plain and unadorned shirt of mountain-sheep skin, buckskin leggings reaching from ankle to waist, and a pair of moccasins Shell herself had worked on for days, and shyly handed to him. There was a nondescript red blanket, also. God, he was glad he could not see himself in this clownlike getup, glad no one in the Eighth Infantry could see him, either!

But he felt pretty well. His eyes healed, some flesh returned to his narrow bones. There had been, too, the beginnings of communication.

↔

Fox Dancer was demonstrating the surveyor's transit to his uncle. The red-haired prisoner had finally managed to explain to Fox Dancer how it worked and what it was for. But Blue Horse was puzzled.

"What good is that round thing on top?" the chief asked. "What good is it if the little arrow always points to the same direction? Who cares about that?"

On a December afternoon they sat alone in the great council lodge. Wind snarled about the *tipi* and the fire flared high, then became smoky and guttering from the gusts that rippled the skins of the lodge.

"If you want to go in a certain direction," Fox Dancer said, "this little arrow always points that way."

"If I want to go in a certain direction," Blue Horse grunted, "I just look up at the Broken Back Star. That guides me."

"But suppose it is daytime. You don't see stars in the daytime."

Blue Horse was fond of his nephew, but this was going a little too far.

"Well," he said, "I know this country. It is my land. I was born here. I know where to go."

Fox Dancer nodded. Diplomatically, he turned to the shiny brass barrel that topped the tripod. "And this thing here. You can look through it, and see things that are far away."

His uncle waved the eagle-feather stick. "I have seen things like that at Fort Jackson. Like two bottles stuck together. The officers looked into them. But if you have good eyes you do not need anything to look through. It is just that those white men have weak eyes, and do not see very good."

"Perhaps it is so," Fox Dancer admitted, adding, "The white man told me they can use this three-legged thing to measure the land." He made the sign; index fingers held together before him, then pulled apart.

Blue Horse stared, incredulous.

"What?"

Fox Dancer repeated his words and made the sign, feeling uneasy. His uncle had stomach trouble, and was sometimes quickly irritable.

"Measure the land?" Blue Horse was thunderstruck. "How do the white men measure the land?"

"I think," Fox Dancer said, "they—"

"Measure the land?" Blue Horse got up from his buffalo robe and stamped about the *tipi* in a comic dance, waving his eagle-feather stick and laughing. "Who can measure the land?" He wiped his eyes with his fringed sleeve.

"But—"

"Everyone knows," Blue Horse said, "that the land goes on forever and forever. True, a mother can measure a child's waist, and make a belt for it. A woman can measure salt into the pot— one, two, three spoons. But measure the land?" He chuckled, sitting down again. With a wave of the stick he signaled to Fox Dancer to put the transit away. "Anyway, I do not like to look at it," Blue Horse grumbled. "I think it is maybe an evil god, like Lightning Man says. I do not want it standing there, looking at me with that shiny glass eye." While Fox Dancer was folding the legs and putting the instrument away his uncle went on, speaking thoughtfully, "Maybe there is more to that thing than you know, nephew. The white men are pretty smart. Maybe that little arrow can point to the truth, instead of just to the north. Maybe with that shiny brass tube they can see far away into the days to come. Not just things a long *way* off, but things a long *time* away. Maybe that is what they have *really* got there, and you just do not know how to use it. But I still do not like to have it around me." He jabbed the stick menacingly at the transit. "Aagh!"

Fox Dancer decided his uncle was probably right. Measure the land? That sounded funny. No, Duffy had probably been afraid to admit the real power of the three-legged god, a Hat People god which was now lost to them. It was medicine, surely it was medicine; in some yet unclear way it must be magic.

In the afternoon the wind died down. Snow fell in huge, flat flakes that were soft on the cheek. At sundown Fox Dancer, strolling through the camp, caught a glimpse of a blanket-wrapped figure standing near the *tipi* where Shell lived with her father, Elk River. Though the face was hidden in the folds of the blanket, Fox Dancer knew who it was. Lightning Man was courting Shell. With a willow flute his cousin was playing an age-old song to his love:

> *Come out, come out.*
> *I stand here making music.*
> *Come hear my music, see me.*

Since the cousins had returned from the buffalo hunt, they had put aside their quarrel. Slyly Fox Dancer crept up behind the flute player, then jumped into view. "Here I am! I hear your music! What do you want, sweet-as-sugar man?"

Lightning Man was angry. He gave Fox Dancer a shove that sent him sprawling in the snow. "What are you doing here? You must have something better to do than to stand around and bother a man! Go away, now! No one asked you to come here!"

Shell, peeking through the tent flap, giggled. Lightning Man rushed away, confused and unhappy. Fox Dancer was sorry he had so angered his cousin. But he stopped in the falling snow long enough to talk to Shell.

Instantly she was shy again, with downcast eyes. "He is well," she murmured. "Almost well, anyway. He is unhappy, though. I think he wants to go back to the fort, and is mad at the snow."

"His name is Duffy," Fox Dancer told her.

Shell looked up, intrigued. "Duf-fy?" She made it two long syllables.

"Duffy."

Again she giggled. "That is a funny name." She tried it again. "Duf-fy. Duffy." Laughing, she said it again and again. "Duffy. Duffy. Duffy!"

Soon they were both laughing. It sounded so silly, that name. When he went away she was still standing in the doorway, one hand holding the flap, experimenting with the queer name.

The winter wore on. Duffy wondered why they had not gone about the torture, killed him, made an end to it. This was worse than being in prison. At Fort Jackson now there would be Christmas festivities. He had lost track of dates, but about now there would be exchanged dinners, decorating of trees, rum punch and conviviality, a holiday dance with much demand for the attendance of bachelor officers. Rooms would be warm, fragrant with the smell of pies baking and preserved oranges and citron chopped up for fruitcakes. In the bachelor officers' quarters the fresh-cheeked younger men would be clumsily wrapping presents that had taken two months to reach the post from Chicago and St. Louis; tortoise-shell combs, a watch with a black ribbon and a jeweled clasp for the bosom, maybe even French scent, cologne water . . .

Cross-legged in the *tipi*, washing his hair from a tin basin, he raised his head, scrubbing grated, milky root-soap into it with his fingers, and sniffed the air. Scent—a woman's scent. How long had it been since he had sensed it warm and musky in his nostrils? He needed a woman. Sweet Jesus, he needed a woman!

There were, of course, compensations to captivity. He learned,

in conversation with Shell, Man-Who-Never-Walked, Twin
Woman, and the young Fox Dancer, a considerable amount of
this spoken language. At Trinity College he had been an honors
student in French and Latin. In this savage camp he began to
recognize strange linguistic structures; to learn the way the
Sioux handled their verbs and prepositions, to commit to memory long strings of the common names for things. *Tollo* was
beef, sugar was *chahumpiaska,* wild mushrooms (which they
dug and dried for winter) were a jawbreaking *yamanuminnig-
awpa,* as nearly as he could pronounce it. From the lissome
young Shell he also made a beginning with their elaborate and
graceful sign language. At first she laughed at his gestures, mim-
icking him with her own fluent and graceful signs. But after a
while he became fairly adept. The sweeping poetry of it stirred
the Gael in him.

From Man-Who-Never-Walked Duffy learned about the cus-
toms and practices of The People, as they always referred to
themselves. He learned about their sixteen great gods—Sun,
Thunder, Rock, and the rest. He learned the markings the
Oglalas painted on their horses. A straight horizontal line, dripping red, meant an arrow wound; a red dripping disk, a bullet
wound. A red hand meant that an enemy had actually touched
the horse. Stripes painted on the right fore leg signified that the
owner had struck enemies on that side, one stripe for each happening. And the ever present eagle feathers in the coiffures of
the men had equally complicated meanings. The first coup permitted the wearer to stick an eagle feather straight up in the
back hair; the second slanted upward toward the right, the third
horizontally to the right, the fourth sloped down toward the
right. Duffy was a good student, remembering all these things.
And Man-Who-Never-Walked was a patient and good-humored
teacher; Duffy got along famously with him and Twin Woman
and Shell.

One cold day, restless from confinement, he put on his
blanket and went out. The sky was lowering and gray, an iron-
hard smell to the air boded snow. Around the camp the pines
stood stark and black, deep shadows within their ranks. A single,

broad stroke of lemon-yellow to the west cut across the gun-metal clouds, the remnant of a December sun. Few people were outside the warm *tipis*, but when the children saw Duffy, they passed the word, shrieking and giggling. In a few minutes there was a merry band at his heels.

"Go away!" he shouted in English, and made malevolent faces. "Go away, you spalpeens, before I call The Black Dog on you!"

It was a game they played, and they were convulsed with laughter. In snow that came to his knees they crowded about, pulling at his blanket, demanding his attention. At first the parents had not liked this, and called the children away. Now, however, they appeared more tolerant, watching him through a pulled-aside door flap.

"All right!" he groaned in mock anger, taking the home-made harp from the folds of the blanket. "All right, you little bastards! I'll play you a tune!" He shook his finger threateningly at one tiny, round-eyed boy. "But only one, mind you! I'm saving my voice for a grand concert at the Philharmonic Society next week!"

Wriggling with delight, they sat on a fallen log and became silent and attentive as young owls. Duffy strummed the harp, singing *mi-mi-mi-mi*. From a buffalo horn softened in boiling water, and sinew taken from a half frozen deer haunch, he had, with help from Shell, fashioned a rude approximation of an Irish harp. It was horribly off tune, and there was no way to adjust the pitch without tying and retieing knots in the sinew. But what the harp lacked he made up for with a loud tenor voice:

> "*I'll eat when I'm hungry, I'll drink when I'm dry*
> *If hard times don't kill me, I'll live till I die.*
> *I'll tune up my fiddle and rosin my bow*
> *And make myself welcome wherever I go.*
> *Sometimes I drink whisky, sometimes I drink rum,*
> *Sometimes I drink brandy, at other times none.*"

Strumming a clangorous chord on the harp, he roared out the chorus:

> *"Rye whisky, rye whisky, rye whisky, I cry!*
> *If you don't give me rye whisky, I surely will die!"*

At the post he had always been in demand for parties with his mandolin. In this godforsaken, savage camp he was still a success. They yelled and screamed and giggled, crying *"Hau, hau!"* to signify applause.

"Well," Duffy said, "I'm damned if it was all that great, but here's another you might enjoy, you snot-nosed little beggars!"

Even some of the women, now, emerged from the *tipis*, and stood listening.

For a moment Duffy stared at the broad lemon-yellow streak in the sky. It was rapidly fading, and in the space where it had been winked a solitary star. A bright star. Perhaps a planet? Or —another star? One that shone a long time ago?

He sang low and sweet, voice husky with remembrance:

> *"Silent night, holy night.*
> *All is calm, all is bright."*

He didn't know where the words came from. It had been so long. But somehow he knew them all, remembered them, felt them familiar on his lips:

> *"Round yon virgin mother and child*
> *Heavenly hosts sing alleluia."*

From somewhere snow began to fall, a gentle drifting down of cottony flakes. One little girl brushed snow from her cheek with a quick gesture, and the others looked at her and then at Duffy again. An Indian woman adjusted the blanket over her head, and might have been a madonna in a church picture.

> *"Christ, the savior, is born—born.*
> *Christ, the savior, is—bornnnnnnn!"*

He held that last note a long time, as if relinquishing something he might never see again.

After he finished, the children were sober. They had sensed the feeling in Duffy's voice. It was a mystical communion that made them quiet, contemplative, almost orderly. A woman called, then another. Slowly the children got off the log and trudged away, one by one. The little girl with the shining eyes stayed for a moment, looking at Duffy with awe. Then she too walked away, to where her mother beckoned.

Later Duffy thought of the incident and was mystified. The red bastards almost seemed to understand him!

If there was some communion between Lew Duffy and a handful of men and women and children in the camp, there seemed damned little with the young Fox Dancer. Duffy was thirtyish, and judged Fox Dancer to be in his middle twenties; a proud, reserved, standoffish type. The slight young man came often to the *tipi* and studied Duffy, saying little. For long periods of time Fox Dancer sat motionless, intent. Occasionally he would ask a question in halting English.

"What white men doing in Oglala land?"

"Surveying for the railroad."

Duffy wondered what in hell the sign for *railroad* was. How describe a locomotive to someone who had never seen one? How make them understand the concept of steel rails, spanning the land?

*Wagon*, he signed, making the prescribed little circles with his forefingers to denote the wheels. They knew wagons. Then *fire*, carrying his partially closed hand well before him, thumb across the nails of his fingers, and snapping the fingers rapidly out; the leaping of flames was suggested. *Fire.* Then the two signs together. *Fire wagon.*

Fox Dancer frowned, intent. Duffy looked around for help, but no one was there. Man-Who-Never-Walked, Twin Woman, Shell; they were gone. When Fox Dancer entered the lodge they left as a sign of deference.

*No horses*, Duffy signed. *No need horses.* "It goes by itself," he finally blurted in English. "They burn wood in the damned things, see? The trains go by themselves, and carry things in cars; cattle, groceries, kegs of brandy, paper collars—whatever people need."

Just when he was giving up, Fox Dancer understood. But his brow wrinkled in disbelief.

"No horses?" he asked in English, incredulous.

Duffy went, on, trying to explain the concept of a railroad. In a stew of English, Sioux, and signs, the two exchanged comments.

"That's right," Duffy concluded. "The railroad is coming. It can't be stopped. It'll bring more goddamned walk-a-heaps than you ever saw. It'll—"

Fox Dancer scowled and raised his hand in a sign. *Wait. Wait.* He held out his hand, fingers extended, and moved it sharply downward. "Slow," he said in English. "Slow goddamn."

Duffy understood. He moderated the quick way he was used to talking. Forming each word slowly and distinctly, he went on:

"You people haven't got a chance. You ought to touch the pen—sign a treaty—the way the President wants you to do. If you don't, we'll just wipe you out, that's all!"

Fox Dancer stared back at him with obsidian-dark eyes when Duffy mentioned the treaty. Seeing he wasn't getting anyplace, Duffy changed the subject.

"Look here, now. I've been doing all the talking." He made signs. *Me. Talk a lot. Now you talk. Why you not kill me?* In English he added, "I'm damned sick and tired of sitting on my arse around here! Pretty soon I'll take root or something and grow into a blasted parsnip! Kill me, goddamnit, or let me go!"

Perhaps Fox Dancer understood more than Duffy thought. At any rate, his eyes showed amusement.

"Do something!" Duffy pleaded. Suddenly he got on his knees and grabbed Fox Dancer's blanket, pulling him close so he could look into the young man's face. "For an active man like me," he shouted, "this is purgatory! Kill me, or let me go!"

Fox Dancer pulled away, drawing his knife in alarm. Remembering he was in a savage camp, the camp of people who had killed most of his command and scattered the rest, Duffy sank back on his heels.

"Well, anyway," he said sulkily, "you ought to tell me *something!*"

A long time passed. Neither seemed aware of the other.

"We watch you," Fox Dancer finally murmured.

"Eh?" Duffy was startled.

Fox Dancer nodded. The single eagle feather standing up from his coiffure made a knifelike shadow against the skin walls of the *tipi.*

"We watch you," he repeated.

Duffy was puzzled. "How do you mean?"

Fox Dancer made the *deer* sign. "Hunt deer. Shoot deer. But first us learn—"

"*We* learn," Duffy corrected.

"We learn deer—" Here Fox Dancer stopped, searching for a word. He made a sign, and Duffy guessed at it.

"Way?" he suggested. "The way the deer—"

"Way!" Fox Dancer said triumphantly. "Learn deer *way.*" He pointed the knife at Lew Duffy. "So. We watch you. We learn you way. We learn white man way. We learn good. Fight him better. So keep you. You—teach us fight white man better."

Duffy sprang to his feet, indignant.

"Is that why you're keeping me? Like a bug stuck on a pin in a natural history class? So *that's* your little game! Sweet Jesus!" Agitated, he began to prowl about the lodge, hands locked behind his back, pausing from time to time to stare at Fox Dancer.

"So that's it! Well, I swear by the Blessed Virgin I'll never tell you one goddamned thing! Do you understand that? I wouldn't give you one murmuring word I ever thought would be used against the Eighth Infantry. Is that clear?"

Fox Dancer seemed amused. Carefully he slipped the trade knife back into the buckskin scabbard at his belt. The handle of the knife held a tuft of hair. It looked like human hair. Duffy looked at the remembered hair, then at the single eagle feather. In a hoarse voice he charged, "You were the one that killed Sergeant Dannaher, back there at the willows! I saw you hit him in the face with your hatchet."

Fox Dancer got up with a quick, elegant movement.

*Finished,* he signed, and drew the door flap aside.

Duffy followed him, insistent.

"Do you hear me?" he demanded. He touched his fingers to his mouth in the sign for *silent,* then *ever and ever.* "Savvy? Understand? I'll never tell you a damned thing!"

Fox Dancer's lips moved in a faint grimace. "You talk," he said. "You always talk. You *need* talk." Then he went out into the winter dusk.

Duffy did indeed need talk, companionship, people around him, drink and fellowship, the soft bodies of women—all the things he had not had for weeks now. It was true. That Fox Dancer was a goddamned smart Indian. But he would never tell the Oglalas anything of military value. Study him, would they? Two could play at that game! He would study *them,* and someday maybe that knowledge would confound the Oglalas, maybe even get Duffy captain's bars! Angry and upset, he strode back and forth for a long time in the narrow confines of the *tipi,* hands locked behind his back, chewing furiously at a corner of his red beard.

One morning, an odd, springlike dawn enclosed in the winter as an island is surrounded by the sea, he came on Shell. The Oglalas wrapped their meat in a buffalo hide, burying it in a deep pit to freeze and surrounding the pit with sticks planted in the ground, each bearing a cloth soaked with wet gunpowder to hide the scent from the wolves. Shell was alone, cutting a steak from an iron-hard carcass.

Duffy helped her. It was warm sitting in the sun, and for the first time in a long while he was content. Shell's voice was soft and low, her black braids shone in the sun, under the deerskin shirt her breasts swelled soft and round.

No one was watching them. He pulled her into the trees, and together they lay on a sun-warmed ledge of rock while he held her to him and enjoyed her.

At first she was surprised, and struggled to escape. But she did not cry out. After a while, feeling his body covering hers, she lay flat against the rock and helped him. A *virgin!* he thought. A *goddamned virgin!*

It was all over quickly. She ran away then, leaving the carved steaks and the knife. Sweet Jesus, he had played the fool again!

*Now* what would they do with him? No more studying a beetle on a pin; this time they would *kill* him! Lightning Man wanted Duffy's hair anyway, and to make matters worse, was sweet on Shell himself. Well, maybe it was better this way, better than rotting in a savage camp. Defiantly he threw the chunk of blood-dripping meat over his shoulder, picked up her knife, and trudged back to the camp.

They didn't kill him. No one said anything about it. Maybe Shell never told anyone.

# CHAPTER FOUR

It was well known that *Wakan Tanka* loved the smell of tobacco. Fox Dancer sat across the fire from his uncle, watching
Blue Horse smoke the white man's Lone Jack. Fox Dancer
sounded out the letters on the sack. Jack, that was a white man's
name. But Lone? He did not know that word.

"Good," Blue Horse grunted. "*Sha, sha.*" He puffed a blue-
gray circle of smoke toward the sooty upper reaches of the *tipi.*
"Is there more?"

Fox Dancer shook his head. "The white man only had this
little sack."

It was the Big-Hoop-And-Stick-Game Month, when children
rolled skin-covered willow hoops down the snowy hills, trying to
stop them by throwing sharpened stick lances. Tobacco was low,
the frozen buffalo meat gone, the Oglalas had eaten most of the
salt beef and flour and beans they had taken at the Battle of the
Willows. Too, the summer-fat camp dogs were gone, long since
made into soups and stews. Now the people were living on a
scanty diet of roots and dried berries, with occasional buffalo or
antelope that wandered too close to the winter-bound camp.

"Bad." Blue Horse sighed, lighting the soggy remnants of
Lone Jack with a coal from the fire. "Very bad. The white man
should have brought more tobacco when he came to fight us."
His face crinkled in a grin.

"He is a brave man," Fox Dancer mused, "and he is truthful,
I think, the way he sees truth. He is foolish, too, and sometimes
says foolish things just to sound brave. A lot of the Hat People
are like that." He made the sign for *white people,* drawing a forefinger across his brow to denote the brim of a hat.

"They are foolish," Blue Horse agreed, "and liars too. But tell me again this crazy thing about a fire wagon."

Fox Dancer did not think Duffy was a liar. He tried to explain, but his uncle was dubious.

"How can it go with no horses?" The pipe had gone out again; when Blue Horse tried to relight it there was only a dry, sucking sound.

Fox Dancer didn't understand, himself. "Well," he said, "there is a fire in it. That is all I know. Duffy says the fire makes it go, faster than a horse can run."

Blue Horse put his pipe away. "I do not think lighting a fire in a wagon can make it go." He nodded toward the meadow where the captured wagon stood, almost covered in drifts of snow. "Do you think you could go out there and light a fire in that white man's wagon and make it go?"

Usually Fox Dancer's uncle scorned fanciful tales. Measure the land? Foolish talk! But this time he appeared almost serious.

"No." Fox Dancer shook his head.

"Then," Blue Horse decided, "let us not hear any more about wagons with fire in them. It takes a horse to pull a wagon. We all know that. *Wakan Tanka* made it so. The white men are just trying to scare us."

As he left his uncle's lodge, Fox Dancer saw Shell and Lew Duffy in the sudden winter twilight. They were across the meadow, near the trees, and walked very close together. The Oglalas were very casual about the matter of sex. They realized a man—even a prisoner—needed a woman now and then. But Shell was Elk River's daughter, and Fox Dancer wished she did not walk so much with Duffy. It looked bad, a scalp-shirt chief's daughter going about with a white man. In this winter season Duffy could be trusted with the run of the camp, though when the snow went they would probably have to tie him up till they were ready to trade him back at Fort Jackson. But Duffy was still an enemy, one of the Hat People. And Shell was high-born, not important in her own right so much as she was a symbol.

The pair moved into the dark shadows of the pines. Annoyed with Shell, Fox Dancer hurried after them. At the edge of the trees he paused, hidden behind a snow-frosted trunk. In the gloom a shadowy figure stalked Shell and Duffy, walking quickly and carefully in their tracks, but keeping out of sight.

When the pair walked back it was fully dark. Fox Dancer remained hidden; when the unknown pursuer came abreast of him, he jerked aside the blanket and caught the man's wrist.

"You!"

Lightning Man was embarrassed and angry. Jerking his hand away, he snarled like an animal. "What are you doing?" Then he drew himself up defiantly, adjusting the folds of his blanket. "I am watching them, that is all. You know Elk River promised Shell to me someday. Already I have horses to give him, good horses, and beads: a lot of things. Elk River wants a lot of things because Shell is pretty. Well, she is promised to me, and I do not like that ugly red-hair man to walk around with her!"

Fox Dancer wanted to poke fun at his cousin but this was no laughing matter.

"Then tell her," he advised, "to stay out of the *tipi* of Man-Who-Never-Walked. Tell her not to cook nice things for the red-hair man anymore. Tell her not to talk to Duffy, to stay away and attend to a woman's business in her father's lodge."

Lightning Man glowered. "I did! But she laughed at me, said I was jealous!" Angrily he broke off an ice-sheathed twig and chewed at it.

"Maybe," suggested Fox Dancer, "you could talk to Elk River. Maybe he would tell Shell not to walk around with the red-hair man."

Lightning Man spat out remnants of the twig. "No! I am not a man who goes around whining like a whipped dog. I will take care of this my own way."

In the light of the yellow moon just rising over the piny spikes to the east he strode away, moccasins making black prints in the snow.

Duffy lay naked and warm in his buffalo robes. Man-Who-Never-Walked and Twin Woman slept on the other side of the dying fire, the old man snoring in a series of groans and wheezes, his wife in a high-pitched staccato.

It had taken him time to get used to sleeping naked, but they all did it; it made sense. Vermin were a problem, vermin in the clothing, especially in winter, when there was no opportunity to wash clothes in the stream. Sleeping naked helped keep lice out of the buffalo robes.

Far away a wolf howled, then another and another. The shrill keening made Duffy restless. Shivering, he slipped from the robes and went to stand at the door flap, peering into the night. Through that notch in the hills under the bright star that shone blue and hard, was Fort Jackson. Once-frozen fingers and toes tingled with the remembrance of the time he tried to run away. Oglalas had brought him back, to be a beetle on a pin. To have taken all that trouble, they must be serious about learning from the white man.

Trembling, half from cold and half from frustration, he laced the flap shut and wriggled back into the robes. My God, the Army was all wrong about this Indian business! Chase the red bastards up hill and down dale all summer, that was the Army way! But when winter came and the Sioux were hidden in retreats like this, what did the blasted Army do? Why, they went to ground too, digging into barracks for the winter! Now *that* was no way to bring the Sioux to heel! The way to handle Sioux was to come after them in the winter, when they were helpless against attack, tied to camp by their stores of food. A camp like this, now— He propped himself on his elbows and stroked his red beard. Man-Who-Never-Walked and Twin Woman still snored; the eye of the fire blinked as a last flame caught, flared up, then smoked out.

A *camp like this* . . .

He finally slept. Late in the morning he woke to find Shell bending over him, teasing with a cup of coffee under his nose. Coffee had been scarce; he wondered where she'd gotten it.

"Thank you, love," he said, sitting up and taking the battered tin cup.

She sat on her legs before him, watching, eager to please. Though Duffy tried, Shell had not learned much English. Fox Dancer, now; the young man was growing more expert in English than Duffy was in Sioux. But Shell did not go much beyond *love* and *dear* and other homely phrases.

"Eat?" she asked. A fresh fire was lighted, and food bubbled in a smoke-blackened pot. Twin Woman and Man-Who-Never-Walked were gone on business of their own.

He pulled her down to him and dragged her within the robes. Her skin was soft and warm, fragrant with sweet grass and smoke. Giggling, she tried to escape but his arms only tightened. *Red or white,* he thought. *They're all alike, aren't they? What's the sin?*

↔

Winter crept interminably on. Food grew scarce, then more scarce. The Oglalas were reduced to slaughtering some of their prized horses. Smaller children died, and there was a brief epidemic of coughing sickness that killed several old people. Firewood was low, the snow so deep it was hard to cut any and bring it to the camp. Duffy went out with a wood party, and froze his fingers and cheeks again. But somehow the camp prevailed. Almost with a will of its own, a collective resolve, life persisted. The processes making up the whole of existence seemed to slow, falter, come near stopping, but life prevailed.

Duffy was bored. Though at first he resented Fox Dancer's nosy interest in him—where he came from, how much money he was paid, why he fought—he now welcomed the visits as a diversion from the snowbound hours. Perhaps they were both bored; after a time there came restrained friendship.

"Fox Dancer," Duffy commented one day. "That's a very peculiar name, you know. How does a man get a name like that?"

They were sitting in the *tipi*, close together near a few red coals. There was no wind; for once, the skin walls of the *tipi* did not ripple and flap and complain. But with the wind gone, the cold was even more of a presence. It lay all around—waiting, powerful, pervasive. Somewhere in the rim of trees bordering the camp another tree popped; Duffy started at the jagged noise.

"I said," he insisted, "what does *Fox Dancer* mean?"

Fox Dancer wrapped himself tighter in the blanket and stared

into the coals. His English was fast improving. There was even a
faint Hibernian tinge to certain words that Duffy was amused
to speculate came from his own way of speaking.

"We dream," Fox Dancer finally murmured.

"Dream, eh? Well, I dream too, but my name's not Phil the
Fluter or the Red-Nosed Leprechaun!"

Fox Dancer explained that when very young he had had a
strong dream. He was walking past a grove of cottonwoods when
a fox saw him and invited him within. There, in the green confines of the grove, a band of foxes was dancing. He was, he said,
invited to join them and learn the intricate steps they favored.
But when he was giddy from too much spinning and whirling,
they started to attack him because he had learned their secrets,
and he barely escaped with his life.

"So," he explained, "I the Fox Dancer. Clever, quick, like
Fox."

He said these last words so casually that Duffy was nettled.

"Well, that isn't so much!" the Irishman snorted. "You ought
to know *you're* talking to a Duffy from County Monahan! Duffy
is *Dubhthaigh* in Gaelic, not that an ignorant savage like you
would know Gaelic from fiddle-dee-dee. And do you know what
*Duffy* means?"

Fox Dancer only looked at him. Whether he understood all
Duffy was saying, the Irishman wasn't sure.

"The Irish," Duffy went on, "had names long before you
heathen stopped crawling and got up on your feet. Black Man
of Peace, that's what *Dubhthaigh* means." He sat back on his
heels, satisfied with himself. "My very cousin—my father's
brother's sister's something or other, I don't recall the exact re-
lationship, was Charley Duffy, that founded *The Nation* and was
tried for treason with McConnell. And you might like to know
this too, young man! Some say Charley Duffy was descended
from King Brian Boramha himself, and so am I then!"

Fox Dancer listened impassively but his eyes betrayed interest. Finally he said, "You not black. You red." There was a
mocking light in his eyes. "Peace? Man of Peace? You?"

"It's a job I do, that's all. Where's a scholar to find his day's bread now? The Army, that's all there is." Having exhausted the subject, Duffy turned to another.

"Is it like this every winter?" he asked, blowing on his fingers. "I mean—life so hard and all? No meat, no fire?"

Fox Dancer nodded. Slight as he was, the youth had lost weight. His face was cut by sharp planes, and skin stretched taut over his high cheekbones. He would be like that, dignified and reserved, Duffy thought, even when dying.

"But you're starving!" Duffy remembered the potato famine of his youth. He had been a child, then; in all of County Monahan not a potato to be had. "Sweet Jesus, it's worse than Ireland in forty-nine!"

Fox Dancer showed a flicker of interest. "Ire-land?"

"Where I was born," Duffy explained, waving his arm. "Back there. A long way back. Across the big waters."

"What you do then?" Fox Dancer asked.

"Starve," Duffy shrugged. "Pray a little. Then starve some more." Maybe that was why he had always been small; there were so few potatoes.

"We same," Fox Dancer agreed. "*Wakan Tanka* hear us soon, and help. No worry."

Duffy was annoyed at the grammar. "*Don't* worry!" he shouted. "Can't you remember a damned thing? It's the imperative form of the verb!"

Fox Dancer smiled. "God-damn," he said, "don't yell me!"

Duffy had to smile, too.

"All right," he agreed. "I'm sorry. You can yell at me when you want to. I don't mind. I had a wife once, for a little time, and she used to—to . . ." Staring into the smoldering fire, he picked up a twig and stirred the ashes. After a while he said, "Speaking of women, I don't see you courting any around here."

"Courting?"

"Means—well, walking out with a girl. Telling her you love her. Sneaking a kiss once in a while. Have you got a girl?"

Fox Dancer wrapped his arms around his knees, drawing closer to the fire. "Maybe. Someday."

"I always figured," Duffy reflected, "it was best to grab the nearest one. Who knows—tomorrow you might be dead!"

"There is time," Fox Dancer murmured. "First, important things to do."

Duffy grinned and knuckled his red hair, now long enough to fall over his shoulders. "What's more important?"

Fox Dancer was serious. "No good tell you," he said. "But listen. My father was scalp-shirt man. He told me what is important. When you go on the warpath, look out for the enemy, do something brave. Study everything, try to understand it. Know the earth, and respect it. Have goodwill to your people. Don't tell lies; a man who lies is weak, like a woman. Don't get mad with anybody, never be stingy. Keep your horses. Then you can give a foal to a man who needs one. That is what I have to do, all those things. They come first, then time to have a woman."

Duffy grinned. "By God!" he blurted, "you're beginning to speak the King's English! I don't mean the sentiments—I don't agree with them at all—but you put the words together very well!" Lacing his fingers around his knees, he rocked back and forth, staring at the fire. Finally, almost unaware of Fox Dancer, he said softly, "Women, that's the thing. That's the only thing. Women, and—"

"The earth," Fox Dancer said, "is my woman. This earth." He touched the ground. "My earth. Oglala earth! But you do not understand that."

Duffy seemed not to have heard.

"Women," he murmured. "And silver eagles. My God, but it would be nice to have silver eagles someday. Imagine that! A poor boy from County Monahan, and silver eagles!"

Incredibly, spring arrived one day. It was a long time coming, but a warm breeze sprang up and some of the waist-deep snow melted. The south wind was a sign of spring to the Oglalas, but it had its bad side, too. The sudden warmth meant more sickness, and people died of a quick fever and loosened bowels. But the rest, made hardy by winter privation, survived.

The sap rose in Duffy as it did in the trees. Now that the

snows were melting, the Oglalas assigned him a guard, a foolish and good-natured brave named Goosey. He followed Duffy about, an ancient musket over his shoulder, important at his task. But Goosey was no bar to escape; he was as charmed by Lew Duffy as the children were, and could easily be diverted. So Duffy lusted for escape almost as he did for Shell. Now that winter was passing, the camp more open, Duffy and Shell had to be very circumspect about their meetings. Too many people were watching. At times his loins ached for her, but Goosey would be watching and he would have to cool his ardor. Lightning Man, especially, seemed to begrudge privacy for Lew Duffy and Shell. He was always sniffing around, watching, glowering.

There came The Moon When The Geese Lay Eggs. The Oglala camp became a wilderness of mud. Children ran shrieking and screaming in muck, splattering anyone who came near. Green shoots poked through winter-killed grass, birds sang, the sky was snowdrifted with clouds. Old men sat in the sun, warming their bones; women broke the ice in the stream and beat clothing against rocks with wooden paddles. Of course, no one really trusted this early spring. The Winter God could strike again, without warning. But they were grateful for sun, for warmth, for renewal of life. It would soon be time for the Willow-Shoot Dance, and the women could go out to dig wild onions. All the Oglalas craved the taste of onions.

Bear Tooth, the shaman, went by. Seeing Duffy cross-legged in the sun, squinting at the horse corral and planning his escape, Bear Tooth shook his rattle and called out a curse. The shaman had been gathering sacred grasses and drying them in the new sun. When he had enough, he would make a small hut, like a sweat bath, and go inside for three days, steeping in smoke from the burning grasses. In that way he would have a good dream to guide the Oglalas during the coming year. The white man, Bear Tooth had decided, was evil. The shaman tried to convince Blue Horse and Elk River, but they were not interested. Now, in his medicine dream, he was going to find out the truth. His private belief was that the Irishman had been sent down by *Iktomi,* the trickster god, to bring trouble, and he regretted his earlier opinion to preserve Lew Duffy.

"Go on!" Duffy called. "Get along with you, you old devil! Don't be going about casting spells on your betters!" He threw a clod at Bear Tooth, and the shaman hurried away, muttering curses.

Lew Duffy had been a lieutenant too long. A war was going on back east. The war, he thought. That's where captains' bars hang on trees, and if a man's got a good reach, he might grab a set of oak leaves. Of course, escape would be difficult. Most of the Oglalas seemed to have accepted Duffy as part of the common furniture of the camp, but they did not often let him out of sight. So there was risk. But what the hell! War was risk; Lew Duffy was a soldier.

One night he and Shell were sitting on a blanket in a grove of budding cottonwoods. The air was warm, fragrant with the smell of small white flowers dotting the meadow. In the shadows an owl hooted, and Shell clung to him, her head on his chest. The Oglalas believed owls were not natural birds, like the magpie or jay or eagle, but rather the ghosts of people who had died of snakebite.

"It's all right," Duffy soothed. "Just a plain, common owl. No reason to take a fright, love."

The owl came closer, or so Duffy thought. At any rate, he heard a rustling in the leaves. *Goddamned bold owl*, he thought. Comfortingly he held her in his arms. Though it was dusk, almost dark, he rested his eyes for a long moment on her face, not quite knowing whether he was seeing or remembering the smooth brow, the delicately chiseled nose, the luminous eyes.

"You're pretty," Duffy said. "Once I knew a girl at home looked a little like you. Her skin was white—white as fresh milk —but she—"

He stiffened. Owl? A twig cracked.

Throwing Shell aside, Duffy rolled away just as the downward-plunging knife buried itself, guard-deep, in the blanket. Lightning Man pulled it free, and leaped again, knife poised.

"You bastard!" Duffy cried, astonished.

Lightning Man rushed again. Shell started to scream, then strangled the cry. She did not want attention from the camp. Letting his assailant come, Duffy rolled away at the last moment, tripping Lightning Man. The knife drove past his ear.

The Irishman had learned streetfighting in Dublin. Snatching the blanket, he whipped it in the air till it wrapped around his forearm like a shield. When Lightning Man rushed again, Duffy grappled with him. Though not tall, nor heavy, the Irishman was wiry and hard. He grunted with the shock of Lightning Man's attack, but held. One hand locking the youth's fingers, the other staving off the knife, he teetered for a moment, then got a toe behind Lightning Man's ankle and tripped him. As they fell, locked together, Duffy knew it was all over. He had lost Lightning Man's knife hand, and so he stiffened his body against that slippery glide of a blade into his belly. But when the knife descended he managed to catch it in the folds of the blanket wrapped about his arm. It cut his arm, he knew, but his belly was whole.

Gritting his teeth, he twisted Lightning Man's hand, knowing satisfaction as the fingers broke, one by one. At the same time, he flailed out with his free arm. The knife, caught in the folds of the blanket, clattered onto a rocky ledge. Shell ran quickly forward to pick it up.

"You bastard," Duffy panted. Struggling for breath, he swayed to his feet. Lightning Man crouched before them, teeth bared like the fangs of an animal. He held the injured hand in his other, looking at Shell. He did not seem to care about Duffy.

"*Wit-ko-win*," he said to Shell.

She flinched, but said nothing.

"*Wit-ko-win*," Lightning Man repeated.

Duffy took the knife from Shell's nerveless fingers. Sticking it in a crack in the ledge, he pulled hard and snapped off the point. Throwing it down between them, he said to Lightning Man, "Get out of here! Now go on with you, you murdering sod!"

When Lightning Man walked away, still holding his broken fingers, Duffy again took Shell into his arms. She was trembling, but, Duffy guessed, not from fear.

"Don't worry," he soothed. "It'll be all right. You'll see, love."

He did not know if it would be all right. But one thing he did know. He knew what *wit ko win* meant. It meant *whore*.

↔

The Oglalas were low on lead and powder and caps. The last coffee bean had long since been ground, brewed, and rebrewed till the product was discolored water. While the hunting was now improving, the long, hard winter had left the animals lean and stringy. They wanted fat, salt pork now, and flour and coffee and other good things.

Travel fever was on them, too. After the hard winter camp, they wanted to get out and around, see the land, smell the new air, get ready for the ritual of their summer fight with their hereditary enemies, the Crows. What better solution to both problems than to take their prisoner now to Fort Jackson and see what could be gotten for him in trade?

Duffy, Goosey at his heels, was standing by the brush corral, eyeing a likely painted pony—small, short-coupled, deepchested —when Fox Dancer spoke. The white man looked around, startled.

"We go tomorrow," Fox Dancer repeated.

"Go?" Duffy looked puzzled. "Go where?"

"To Fort Jackson."

"You're taking me back?" He seemed unable to grasp the situation.

Fox Dancer nodded.

"Guess you got all you could out of me," Duffy decided, and added, "not that it was much."

No one had told Duffy that he was now trade goods. It was a kind of joke with the Oglalas; they all looked forward to seeing his face when they told him he was to be bartered for a few sacks of tobacco. They expected, of course, to get a great deal of merchandise for him, but they wanted to have some fun.

The party was quickly made up. Blue Horse, suffering from his bad stomach, decided not to go. Lightning Man's injured fingers were in considerable pain, and he was spending a large part of each day with his hand soaking in hot sage water; he could not pull a bow. Elk River did not like to go to the fort. Every time he went, they wanted him to touch the pen—sign a treaty—and it made him angry. He was growing old and crotchety, and wondered why they did not leave him alone.

Fox Dancer, Blue Horse suggested, was a promising young man, wise for his years, and behaved bravely in fights. Besides, Fox Dancer had learned a lot during the winter from the red-hair man, and could now speak tolerable English. He was young, that was true, but dependable and cautious. So it was decided that Fox Dancer would lead the party, bargain with Colonel Forsythe for the release of Duffy, and bring home a lot of good things.

"Tobacco," Blue Horse reminded him. "Plenty of tobacco."

"Yes," Fox Dancer agreed.

"What do they call it?"

"Lone Jack!"

"Yes."

Most of the party were middle-aged—people like Little Man and Scraper, Goosey, Black Mouse, No Neck. But they deferred to Fox Dancer. The young man was Blue Horse's nephew, and Blue Horse was very respected. Too, Fox Dancer had performed well at The Battle of the Willows. Then, everyone knew that the young man had in his lodge a powerful god of the white men that he had captured, and that from time to time he consulted it and it told him magic things.

They went off in a long file, fifteen of them, Scraper proud at being assigned to carry the transit in the hide case Twin Woman had sewn for it. Fox Dancer rode in the post of peril, at the end of the column. Lew Duffy, loudly objecting, rode beside him, tied by a stout buckskin rope around his waist to Scraper and the transit. The Oglalas did not want him to run away.

For three days the party rode through a harsh country now softened by the bloom of spring. Snow was still on the peaks, and even in foothills not far above their heads. But the sun was warm, yellow and white and pink flowers spangled the new grass. Melting snow made the streams run full and deep, and once Duffy was nearly swept away in a foaming torrent. Only the rawhide rope securing him to Scraper saved him.

For three days they rode, in no hurry, until at last they broke out on a rocky escarpment above a lush, green valley. In the distance, Fox Dancer pointed out, was Fort Jackson. Duffy could not make out the post, but he whooped with relief, kneed his pony so that it pawed the ground and turned skittish.

"What are we waiting for?" he demanded.

They bound his hands and feet and sat him at the base of a tree, where Little Man and Goosey remained to guard him while the others rode on to the post.

"What the hell is this for?" Duffy spluttered, trying to twist free of the rawhide thongs. "Is this any way to treat a friend?"

Fox Dancer sat his pony easily, looking down at Lew Duffy.

"First we go in to post. See what they give for you."

"Give for me?" Duffy spluttered, twisting and kicking. "What in Christ's name does that mean?"

It was the moment they all had been waiting for.

"Oglalas run out of tobacco," Fox Dancer said gravely. "That Lone Jack is good tobacco. You are not worth much, but maybe we can get a few sacks of tobacco for you."

Duffy was furious. "A few sacks of tobacco?" He writhed in his bonds, face red as his hair.

Fox Dancer grinned. "You skinny. Ugly! Look like dog meat! Maybe Colonel Forsythe throw in a little coffee, too, but I don't think so."

As the young man spoke he signed his words, too, and the Oglalas burst into laughter, slapping bare thighs, giggling, pounding one another on the back. In their way, they liked Duffy; they did not joke with someone they did not like.

Lew Duffy did not disappoint them. When Fox Dancer looked back Duffy was rolling on the ground, cursing, trying to break his bonds. Goosey and Little Man were having a good time, poking their fingers at him and laughing. Fox Dancer suspected that Duffy was praying to the Hat People gods. At any rate, the Irish man was howling, "Sweet Jesus, sweet Jesus, sweet Jesus!"

# CHAPTER FIVE

Fort Andrew Jackson was situated near the forks of the Platte. Built to protect emigrant trains traveling the Platte Road to the riches of the newly opened Northwest, it was now, because of the war, reduced to three companies of the Eighth Infantry.

A log stockade, ten feet high, surrounded the post. Inside was a cluster of warehouses, barns, now only half-occupied barracks for troops, and a large house with a veranda for the commanding officer, Lieutenant Colonel Eben Forsythe. There was a steam sawmill, also, but in that country trees were scanty; most of those near the post had been cut down to build the stockade and barracks. Even for firewood, it was necessary to send wood parties as much as ten miles distant.

Forsythe was a terrierlike veteran of the Mexican War, and had lost an arm at the Battle of Chapultepec, where General Pillow himself had commended him for gallantry. Now, grizzled and restless, he had been recalled to this frontier post to hold the Sioux in check till the war was over. It was a dull and thankless job.

Strolling the parapet on a spring-scented morning, he was perplexed to see the mangy "hang-around-the-fort" Indians scatter, hurrying this way and that, huddling against the stockade walls as if for protection.

"Hand me my glasses," he ordered his adjutant.

Through the fieldglasses the colonel saw a long file of Sioux approaching from the southwest.

"By God!" he muttered.

"What is it, sir?" the fresh-cheeked adjutant inquired.

Forsythe kept his eyes glued to the glasses. Could it be?

"Sir—" the adjutant said.

"Shut up, will you?" Forsythe snapped. By God, there they were, at last; the real hard-cases! It had been a long time since Forsythe had seen real Sioux—warriors like Red Cloud and Elk River and the rest.

"Sir," the adjutant insisted, feeling that he ought to take some part in matters, "shall I muster C Company?"

"You do that, Henry," Forsythe said, and rushed back to the verandaed house to find his dress tunic and his best saber.

Clattering into the house, he called his wife. "They're here!" he cried.

Phoebe had been gardening, planting a Vermont maple tree in remembrance of home. Now she helped him get into his tunic and buckle his sword belt.

"Who's here, dear?"

"From that distance it was hard to tell, but it looked like some of Elk River's Oglalas. Maybe the ones that wiped out the survey party last fall!"

"That's nice," Phoebe said. "Here's your saber, now. Is the belt a little too tight, perhaps?" At the door she suddenly called after him. "But why do you let them come here, after what they've done?"

With a muttered response he hurried back to the parade ground just as the Oglalas rode through the gates.

"C Company all present and accounted for, Colonel," John Logan said, saluting with drawn saber.

Rather than meeting the Sioux afoot, he should have taken time to get his chestnut mare from the stables, but there was no time now. Big men, the Oglalas towered above him, impressive in mountain-sheep skin shirts with trailing fringes, buckskin leggings rich with beadwork, scarlet blankets around their shoulders. They were dressed to the nines; must be something important. Forsythe looked at them with the professional interest of a soldier examining others of his trade. Why do you let them come here, Phoebe had asked, after what they've done? A nice question; why, indeed? But Forsythe was a good officer; he had his orders from the civilian idiots at the Indian Commission back in Washington. Get along with the Sioux, turn the other cheek, try to accommodate! It was enough to make a man puke!

"Stand easy, C Company," Forsythe ordered, and gestured the Sioux delegation toward his office at one corner of the compound.

At his order the adjutant passed around small packets of tobacco. "Now," the colonel said in a brisk tone, "what can I do for you gentlemen?"

Gentlemen? Plumed and beaded assassins!

"Well?" he barked. "Who's the spokesman, eh?"

He should have called John Logan in. Maybe the Oglalas had no English. But more likely it was their way. He recalled Logan's advice: "Never hurry a Sioux. Give them plenty of time. When they're ready they'll talk." Uncomfortably he shifted in his chair. "Here," he said to the adjutant. "Light my damned pipe for me, will you, Henry?" He would just sit and smoke for a while with them, see what happened.

Minutes passed. Five minutes. Ten minutes. The Oglalas puffed in silence. Forsythe could hear the homely sounds of the post through the open window; clanging of hammers from the blacksmith shop, a horse's shrill whinny, the flag whipping on its staff in the fresh spring wind.

"Maybe they've come to talk about signing the treaty," he muttered to Henry. Oglala land lay directly in the path of one of the proposed Central Pacific routes. It would be a fine climax to his career to get the hostiles to touch the pen, agree not to molest the track-laying crews that would come someday soon.

When at last one of the Oglalas spoke, it startled Forsythe. The brave was perhaps the least impressive of the band, a slight young man, simply dressed, with a single eagle feather in his black locks contrasting with the rich dress and ceremonial ornaments of the others.

"I am Fox Dancer," the young brave announced. "My uncle Blue Horse. Elk River is our chief. We come a long way to see you." One by one he introduced the members of his group— Black Mouse, Scraper, No Neck, others.

The colonel shook hands ceremonially with all of them. Then

there was silence, more smoking. Impatient, Forsythe sucked on his pipe, staring at them. In spite of his youth, the spokesman appeared to be an important man among the Oglalas. And that curious accent in his fluent English—it sounded almost Hibernian!

When the bowls of the pipes were empty, Fox Dancer spoke again. For the benefit of the others, he signed his words as he spoke, a graceful play of long-fingered hands that made Forsythe think of swallows swooping and darting about the post stables.

"We come to trade with you," Fox Dancer announced.

"Eh?" Forsythe was startled.

Fox Dancer nodded. "Trade. We need things."

The colonel laid his pipe on the desk. The post warehouses were nearly empty; the war in the East laid first claim to powder and ball and salt pork and flour and cloth.

"Trade, eh? What have the Oglalas to offer?"

"Duffy," Fox Dancer said. "Trade him for—oh, for black powder, lead, knives."

Forsythe stared. "Duffy?"

Fox Dancer nodded.

"Duffy?" the adjutant asked in a hushed voice. "Lew Duffy? Why, he'd dead."

"Wait a minute," Forsythe said. He gestured with his one hand, trying to cover his surprise. "Duffy? Lieutenant Duffy? A mick? I mean—an Irishman? Red hair?"

Fox Dancer, squatting cross-legged, knocked the dottle from his pipe and looked coolly at the colonel. "Yes. Lew Duffy. Red hair. Irishman. His father was king, he says."

"That's Duffy!" the adjutant blurted. "But—"

"Where is he?" Forsythe demanded.

The young man put the pipe back in the decorated pouch that hung from his belt and took out a painted stick. For some time he scratched pleasurably at his dark braids, then said, "A little way from here. But you never find him, I think. Not till you give us things."

So Duffy had somehow survived the attack on the surveying

party! Warily Forsythe asked, "Is he all right? In good health, I mean? Not injured, or sick?"

Fox Dancer smiled, which annoyed Forsythe. "He is all right," he said.

"How do I know?"

The smile faded. "I only say truth," Fox Dancer said. "Women lie, sometimes. A man does not lie."

This was an amazing turn of events. The bad penny, turning up after all these months! "All right then," the colonel agreed, "what do you want for Duffy?" Quickly he added, before Fox Dancer could speak, "Mind you, I'm almost out of supplies myself. Don't get any grand ideas!"

Fox Dancer had a list. He read off the items; flour, coffee, salt pork, shelled corn, saleratus, dried apples, two kegs of black powder, percussion caps, lead for casting bullets, beans . . .

"Now wait a minute!" Forsythe protested. How much did they think a second lieutenant was worth?

Rice, the young man went on, impassive. Iron kettles, steel needles, calico in bolts, some red blankets . . .

The colonel mopped his forehead. Their demands would come close to emptying his warehouses, and the next supply wagons were not due for another month at least.

"I don't know," he grumbled. "Let me think about this for a minute." Behind his hand he muttered to Henry, "That's one hell of a lot of goods for a second lieutenant. Especially for that goddamned hare-brained Lew Duffy."

The adjutant, like several of the officers at Fort Jackson, never had gotten along well with Lew Duffy. Too high and mighty, and the Irishman bragged too much. Besides, Duffy was a troublemaker, and took their money at cards.

"Yes, sir!" he agreed. "Duffy isn't worth it."

But there could be no question of not redeeming Duffy. After all, he was a white man, and an officer. For the rest of the afternoon the colonel haggled with the Oglalas, but they were persistent, stubborn. Finally Forsythe gave in. His command would just have to go on short rations for a while. Forsythe

shook hands all around, terms finally agreed to. The Oglalas
were shrewd traders.

When the Sioux brought Lew Duffy into the post the following morning, the colonel was still annoyed at the sharp bargain
the Oglalas had driven. The bartered Irishman stood before
him, dressed in outlandish Sioux garb, shifting from one foot to
the other and avoiding his colonel's eye. Finally he blurted,
"Lieutenant Lewis Duffy reporting, sir." When Forsythe's bleak
countenance didn't change, Duffy added, "I—I've been on de-
tached duty, sir."

Forsythe snorted. He walked around Duffy, looking at the
beaded shirt, the high moccasins, the long red hair dressed in a
kind of pigtail with otter skin binding it. "You're a sight," he
growled. "A goddamned sight! Look at you!" Then, in spite of
himself, he began to laugh.

"I didn't think I was so damned funny-looking as all that!"
Duffy protested. "Besides, my clothes wore out. It was a cold
winter, and I had to wear something!"

The Oglalas filed out, some of them grinning too, and went
to camp beyond the stockade in preparation for the delivery of
their goods the next day. Forsythe, striding to the window, saw
the *wagluhke* scatter again as the Oglalas rode out. The beggars
were really afraid of Fox Dancer and his band.

"Well, what happened?" he snapped at Duffy, remembering
that this cocky Irishman had lost an Eighth Infantry command,
a railroad surveyors' party in the bargain, and was now responsi-
ble for seriously depleting Fort Andrew Jackson's scanty supplies.

Duffy gnawed at a corner of his beard. "They jumped us,
thirty or so of them out on a buffalo hunt. First they sent a
party to palaver. They said we were on Oglala land, and to get
the hell out. But one word led to another. The first thing I
knew this big buck drove his pony against me and started to
yell. One of my men—Graham, it was, Corporal Graham, God
rest his soul—got excited and fired. The rest of the Sioux poured
out of the willows, and in a minute it was all over. Privates

Burke and Campbell were all I had left, sir. When I proposed to follow the Oglalas, they deserted."

"I know," the colonel muttered.

"You—you know? Sir?"

Forsythe turned away from the window. "We caught Campbell in a wagon train on the Platte Road. He was headed for Oregon. Told us everything, admitted deserting. But he said the Oglalas killed you. Anyway, we've got him in the guardhouse. Probably hang him soon."

Duffy whistled, and said, "Well, that's all. They caught me, kept me in their camp all winter. Tried to make me give 'em information, but I wouldn't talk, I'll say *that* much."

Forsythe slapped his single hand on the scarred surface of the desk. "You were a goddamned fool, Duffy! I never heard of such a crazy thing! If you'd come back to the post, like a proper Infantry officer, we'd have sent out a force and drubbed them good! As it was, by the time we followed up your tracks and found what was left, it was too late to do anything. The hostiles were long gone, and it was coming winter."

Duffy was sulky. "I didn't want them to get clear away!" he protested. "Besides, I killed several of 'em on my own! If I'd just had a little luck . . ."

Forsythe gnawed at his fist, looking at his lieutenant with baleful eyes. "*Luck!* Good Christ, you damned Irish get a hell of a lot more luck than you're entitled to, seems to me!" He picked up the empty pipe, clamping his teeth hard on it. "By God, I wish I had half your luck, Duffy! I'm tired of minding the store out here while everybody else is back East fighting a war! I'm a clerk for the Indian Commission, that's all. You young fellows are the lucky ones, getting a chance at some action!"

Duffy was puzzled. "Sitting in an Indian camp all winter isn't my idea of action, Colonel."

"I didn't mean that!" Forsythe said. He leaned forward, voice chilly. "I've got a draft to fill, two company-grade officers to send back for duty with the Army of the Potomac. John Logan's one of them. Can't spare him—he knows too much about the

Sioux but I've *got* to release him. Till today, I was strapped to figure out who the other one would be. But you did at least *one* thing right, Lieutenant. You came back just in time!" Forsythe chuckled, a hard chuckle with little mirth in it. "Ransomed from the Red Indians! Trust Duffy to do it with fanfare and trumpets! Anyway, you and Captain Logan will be leaving Friday for the railhead. I'll have your orders made up. Now get the hell out of here!"

Lew Duffy's face hardly contained his elation. He reached out and took the colonel's hand, shaking it vigorously. "I'll be ready, sir!" he cried, and was not embarrassed when Forsythe raised his eyebrows and drew his hand away.

"You don't need to worry about me, sir!" he called from the doorway, and in his anxiety to leave he bumped into a stand and endangered the Boston fern the colonel's wife had installed in the office.

"Good luck," Forsythe said gruffly, and righted the teetering fern. In a way, he was sorry to see Duffy go. But not very sorry. The Irishman was now someone else's problem; all Eben Forsythe had to worry about were hostile Sioux.

←→

Before Duffy left he paid for a large photograph of himself and Fox Dancer standing together before the officers' quarters. Fox Dancer was doubtful, and had to be argued into it. "Look!" Duffy said, exasperated, "it's no different from that transit you stole! It's just a little box on a tripod, that's all. Nothing in it to hurt you!"

Warily Fox Dancer posed for the portrait. But when Duffy attempted to put his hand around his late captor's shoulders, that was too much. The Oglala walked away, sullen, and had to be coaxed back.

"If you don't want to act friendly," Duffy explained, "that's all right. But just stand there, will you, while the photographer mucks about with his hat over the lens." He did not explain that he had a female friend in Washington who would be impressed by a picture of himself standing beside a painted Red Indian. The photograph might impress others, too. In these days, when the Army was commissioning shoe clerks and college students, Lew Duffy's experience should be worth at least a major's gold leaves.

The picture came out well. Duffy gave Fox Dancer a print "To remember me by," he joked.

Fox Dancer stared at the muddy brown of the "picksher." He would not, of course, want to show it to the other Oglalas, but he did roll it carefully. It was still damp from the chemical baths, and he put it in his beaded pouch along with his pipe and tobacco and scratching stick.

"Well," Duffy said, "I guess I'm on my way."

"Where you go?" Fox Dancer asked.

Duffy waved his arm. "Back there. A lot of fighting going on. They need soldiers."

"Who you fight?" Fox Dancer asked, a flicker of interest in his eye.

"Rebs," Duffy said carelessly. "Old Lee and his rebs."

"Indians? Like us?"

Duffy laughed. "No, they're not Indians! They're—" He dug the polished toe of one boot into the ground. "Other white men."

Fox Dancer's face was impassive. But Duffy felt uneasy. "You savages don't understand such things," he explained. "It's a war between the states, see? Old Lee and the rebs are fighting to keep their slaves, and President Lincoln doesn't want—he told 'em they couldn't have slaves, and—well, I mean—" At a loss for words, he broke off and stared defiantly at Fox Dancer. "Anyway," he shrugged, "there's where I'm going. Like Shakespeare said—'seek the bubble reputation in the cannon's mouth.'"

An orderly led up Duffy's horse. The column was ready to escort him and Captain Logan to the railhead.

"I don't understand that," Fox Dancer murmured. He waved to the east. "You go back there. You fight—other white men? Like we fight Crows?"

Duffy swung into the saddle, natty in new blues, auburn locks freshly pomaded.

"I didn't expect you to understand it," he snapped. He put his spurs to the horse and the column trotted away toward the railhead and the war.

While his quartermaster was profanely tallying supplies for the Oglalas the next morning, Colonel Forsythe was surprised to see Fox Dancer enter his office with a peculiar request.

"A railroad train?" the colonel asked, puzzled. "You want to see a picture?" Rummaging in a box, he found a dog-eared copy of *Frank Leslie's Illustrated Newspaper*, several years old. Leafing through it, he located a cut of a 4-4-0 Baltimore-and-Ohio engine pulling a string of freight cars up a grade and chuffing smoke.

"Is this what you mean?"

The young man looked at it and nodded.

While Forsythe went back to work, Fox Dancer squatted in a corner of the office, oblivious to the bustle and confusion. Messengers came and went, officers were summoned for conferences, the details of Private Campbell's execution for desertion in the face of the enemy were settled. Still Fox Dancer sat in the corner, staring at the illustration. Finally he asked a question.

"This is where the fire goes?" he demanded, pointing.

The colonel nodded. "They put wood in there, see? It gets water hot, so that it steams. You know steam?"

"Yes."

"Well, that steam expands—gets bigger, you know. It pushes against a piston, and that—that—" Uneasy under Fox Dancer's fixed stare, he coughed and looked away. "Well, anyway, the fire makes it go."

Morning sun came through the window, bathing Fox Dancer in light. Still he stared at the illustration. Forsythe went home to eat boiled beef and potatoes with his wife, and took a nap. After dinner he returned; Fox Dancer was still looking at *Frank Leslie's Illustrated Newspaper*.

"Seems like that's a goddamned interesting picture," the colonel muttered, by way of starting a conversation. This young man was very shrewd; Forsythe never knew when information would come in handy. But Fox Dancer only looked briefly at the colonel, and went back to the newspaper.

Lights changed, shadows moved, men came and went. Finally the quartermaster entered, saying that the wagon and team the Eighth Infantry had loaned the Oglalas for transport of their booty was loaded. Fox Dancer handed back the newspaper, and together they went out, Eben Forsythe and the young Oglala Sioux. What is he thinking? the colonel wondered. How do such savages think? What do they really think, in the sense that a white man thinks?

Outside the palisade there was anger and frustration among the Oglalas. Black Mouse, rummaging in the wagon, said, "Where are the dried apples? I like dried apples!" Scraper cried, "There is only a little piece of bright cloth! The walk-a-heap chief promised us a big roll of it!" No Neck was very angry. He pointed his musket at the quartermaster sergeant, shouting, "There is only one barrel of black powder! How do you expect a man to fight with no powder? Go and get the other barrel of powder!"

What might have been a bad incident was prevented when Forsythe rushed between them and knocked up the sergeant's pistol. "Just a minute!" he said. "No need for tempers, now!"

Fox Dancer said, "You promised us all these things. We shook your hand, and you shook ours. Where are the dried apples and bright cloth and the gunpowder?"

Forsythe reddened, his short hair bristled. "I think we've been very fair with you," he snapped. "We even threw in the team and wagon, though I doubt we'll ever see either of them again. I'll have to talk to the quartermaster and find a way to survey them." When Fox Dancer didn't speak the colonel went on, his voice rising. "You can't expect us to beggar ourselves, can you? We're on short rations anyway, till the supply wagons get here from the railhead!"

"You promised us these things," Fox Dancer repeated. He was angry, but nothing could be gained by anger. They were three hands of fingers of Sioux amid a hundred or more Hat People. "It is not right!" he insisted. "You shook hands. When a Sioux shakes hands, he always does what he says he will do. What do the Hat People mean when they shake hands?"

The colonel was stubborn. In response to his gesture a dozen armed soldiers came quickly through the stockade gates. A sergeant snapped a salute, saying, "Yes, sir, Colonel."

"You've got all you're going to get," Forsythe said to Fox Dancer. "I'm sorry, but we did the best we could. I hope you'll realize you got a very good bargain, and let it go at that."

The angry Sioux all looked at Fox Dancer. They wanted to fight, whatever the odds.

"I think," Fox Dancer said, "you have cheated us."

Forsythe clenched his fist. "Sergeant," he barked, "dismiss your men!" He walked away across the grass, back to the shelter of the stockade. The soldiers followed, and in response to some unheard order, closed the stockade gate, normally open during the day.

"They are liars, cheats!" Scraper protested. "I told my woman I would bring her bright cloth for a dress! But there is only a little piece!"

Black Mouse looked stricken. "No dried apples," he kept saying. "No dried apples!" Little Neck pointed his gun at the closed gate and shouted, "If anyone comes out now, I will shoot him!" He was very angry.

It took all of Fox Dancer's powers of argument to get them away from the post. The Oglalas still wanted to argue, to threaten, to fight—anything to relieve their feelings. But finally, after a great deal of amused comment from the soldiers standing on the parapet behind the high log walls, he got them on their horses. The team and wagon pulled away toward the camp in the mountains.

A few miles from the post they came on a work party felling trees for the Eighth Infantry mess stoves. Traveling a little below the summit of a long, grassy ridge, the Oglalas were not seen. Quickly Scraper dropped from his pony and ran to the peak of the ridge. Flinging himself into the grass, he steadied his gun, aimed it at the distant wood detail.

As fast as Scraper ran, Fox Dancer was faster. Seeing Scraper's finger tighten about the trigger, he kicked him hard in the face. The gun dropped into the grass while Scraper rolled on the ground in pain, holding his cheek.

"What did you do that for?" No Neck yelled. He dug his heels into his pony's ribs and galloped forward, flinging himself off in anger to confront Fox Dancer. "We should kill them, we should kill them all!" he shouted. "Are we women, that we just let them cheat us and run away like whipped dogs?"

"Yes!" Black Mouse cried. "Why did you hit to my friend Scraper? He was just going to shoot a white man, that is all! Only a walk-a-heap!"

Scraper, recovered, got up and pulled his tasseled knife from its scabbard. "Someone kicked me," he said in a quiet voice. "Someone kicked me in the face. Someone has got to pay for that."

Inside Fox Dancer felt hollow, weak. But he made his voice firm.

"You act like children," he said. "You get mad, yes! You kick and bite and act very brave. You say a lot of fierce words. But what good will it do to shoot a soldier? It is just like a little child biting someone he does not like. No, that is not the way to fight the Hat People! They are very smart. Besides, there are a lot more soldiers back there." He waved to the east, where Duffy had gone. "We have to find some other way."

Still they clamored, wanting to ride around the wood party and ambush it from a grove of cottonwoods that lay nearby. "That will show them not to cheat us!" Black Mouse shouted. "We will teach them a lesson! *Hopo*, brothers—let's go!"

Scraper had a big welt on his cheek where he had been kicked. "First," he said, "my knife wants blood. My knife wants blood to wash out what has happened. I have been kicked, kicked like a dog!"

Fox Dancer hoped they did not see him trembling. Life was sweet, the land was sweet—a lot of things had to be done. But now he did not attempt to protect himself.

"I know what I am talking about," he told them. "The three-legged white god always tells me what to do." He pointed at it in the wagon where, surrounded by sacks and barrels and parcels, it pointed into the afternoon sky like a prophetic finger. "This god," he said, "tells me that to shoot at the white men now is wrong. And that is all I am going to say about it."

Deliberately he turned his back on them and folded his arms, waiting for Scraper or someone to strike from behind, to plunge a knife into his back, simply to shoot him and then rush down the ridge toward the distant wood party. He was very alone, and frightened. Never had he feared the Crows, or the Shoshones, or the Hat People and their walk-a-heap soldiers. But this was different; these were his own people, and he was alone and frightened. No one was here to support him. Not Elk River, not his uncle Blue Horse. No one but himself—and the three-legged god.

After a while, when nothing happened, he got on his pony and started toward the distant Oglala camp. There was muttering, some angry looks, but no one harmed him. They only rode behind, in silence.

# CHAPTER SIX

It was The Moon When Corn Is Planted. After the long winter, the Oglala camp lazed in the genial heat of the sun. In the box-elders and willows along the stream the women washed clothes and gossiped. Meadowlarks sang, the chirping of sunwarmed crickets filled the air. Rattlesnakes began to emerge from winter seclusion, and a group of small boys teased one with a stick, jumping back and squealing with delight when the viper struck at its tormentors.

Now there was food again, plenty of food. The Oglalas built a kind of pound in the river from willow saplings and snared fish. The women dug *pomme blanche* roots and wild turnips in the meadow. Antelope and deer were abundant. Hunting parties brought in a lot of buffalo meat, mostly bull meat; in the late spring bulls were fatter and juicier than cows. Having a particular liking for horse meat, the Sioux killed the horses Colonel Forsythe had loaned them to pull the Army wagon, and feasted. To satisfy the winter craving for sweets there was box-elder sap, boiled into a thick syrup, and young shoots of wild licorice, supplemented with the sugar they had wheedled from Forsythe. Life was good, life was sweet. They felt no enmity toward anyone.

Old Bull Head, the camp crier, made the rounds of the camp, shouting out the news. His voice was so powerful that he said it hurt him. Fingers stuck in his ears, he rode his shambling pony about the camp, starting at the open northern end and taking a long time to make the circuit. There will be a willow dance in the meadow tonight; everybody bring flutes and drums. Badger Man has a son born last night, and is giving away three horses in thanks. Owns Lance Society will have a meeting by the river at sun-overhead-time to see who can throw the farthest.

Fox Dancer, sitting in Elk River's *tipi* with his uncle, Blue Horse, was trying to explain the railroad to the chief. Perhaps the Hat People were just making talk about the railroad, but Fox Dancer did not think so. He spent a lot of time in his own lodge, staring through the telescope of the transit, feeling that perhaps Blue Horse had been right; maybe, if he only knew the secret of the instrument, he *could* see into the future. Maybe the little arrow *did* point to the truth. But so far he had gotten nowhere.

"I do not believe them anyway," Elk River said, puffing contentedly at his pipe, loaded now with a fresh supply of Lone Jack tobacco Fox Dancer had brought from the fort. "I think it is all a lot of talk, just to scare us. Wagons that go without horses—pah!" He spat.

Blue Horse was of two minds. "The railroad thing is hard to believe," he admitted, "but my nephew is wise for his years. He was always different from other boys. He is like his father, who was my brother, always dreaming. And dreams can speak the truth."

Elk River was getting old and crotchety. Sometimes he would become angry for no reason at all. Sometimes, when a man was talking to him, he would doze off and have to be awakened. But he was still the chief.

"All right," he grumbled. "Young man, tell me again what you think. But talk slow and clear. Sometimes I do not hear very well, and I do not want to miss anything."

Fox Dancer shook his head. "You are very wise, Uncle, and I am foolish to argue with you. But suppose what the Hat People say is true. That railroad—" He made the sign now common among them to describe the phenomenon—*fire wagon*. "If it can carry them fast and far, faster and farther than Oglala ponies can run. The fire wagons can carry guns and swords and cannon and powder and all kinds of things. It can—"

He broke off in exasperation and dismay. Elk River was asleep, mouth open, hunched body swaying a little.

"He is tired," Blue Horse said softly. "An old man like him needs a lot of sleep."

"But—"

"For now, it is enough," his uncle said, and left him.

Outside, snowbanks of cloud drifted. Spiky towers of pine pierced the blue, and were tipped with fresh and verdant green. The river laughed over the riffles. In a dammed-up pond a trout jumped, and ever-widening circles honored the also-round sun. The Oglala ponies grazed contentedly in the tender grass, and far to the west, snow-capped, the ramparts of the great mountains reared into the sky.

Fox Dancer was an eloquent young man, a good speaker by all Sioux standards, but this was something he had never been able to put into words or signs, this feeling that made his heart act like it would burst. All this was one, in a mysterious way he could not speak; the sky, the mountains, the river, the birds, the animals, he himself, and all the people, even the feeling in his heart. And maybe—maybe it was well he could not put the feeling into words. Words were for common things—*fire, sugar, finger, baby.* If the things he felt could be put into words, then it too would be common, and he did not want it to be common. Better unspoken, only felt.

But even now there was a cloud. Low on the horizon, out of place in the eye-hurting blue of the sky, was a gathering of darkness, not so much cloud as an inexplicable scaling-down of the day's brilliance. Fox Dancer was watching this place when he became aware of someone looking at him. Turning, he saw Bear Tooth in the shadow of Elk River's lodge.

The shaman shook his rattle at Fox Dancer and made signs of malediction. Now that Fox Dancer's three-legged white man's god had become so well known, Bear Tooth feared competition. His place in the tribe's councils, once secure and unassailable, was threatened.

*Evil!*, the shaman signed. *Your medicine is evil! Rock and the other gods should wipe you out.* He extended his open left hand, rubbing his right palm so vigorously over it that there was a dry, rasping sound. *Wipe you out! You will bring a lot of trouble.*

That was what Lightning Man had said too, when he and his cousin fought that night after the Battle of the Willows. Ordinarily Fox Dancer would have laughed, although politely—a shaman was an important man—and gone about his business. But the trouble was not only Bear Tooth. The shaman and Lightning Man spent a great deal of time together now, making charms and amulets. Fox Dancer had an uneasy feeling about their alliance.

↔

Elk River's band of Oglalas numbered more than a hundred lodges, three hundred warriors, and over a thousand horses. Other, even larger, bands of Oglalas roamed through the hills, and permanent winter camps abounded in the foothills of the mountains. But in spite of its small size, Elk River's band was greatly respected. It had a long tradition of valor and wisdom, and had produced famous leaders. This was an enviable record, considering that the total of Sioux, including the Brulé, the Santee, the Miniconjou, and the rest, scattered widely over Dakota, Wyoming, and Montana, totaled many thousands. But they all—even the poorer and smaller bands, like the Oncpatina and Wahpeton—knew Elk River and his people. The band was, in its way, an aristocracy among the far-flung Sioux; brave in battle, wise in council, magnanimous in victory, in defeat patient and enduring.

That summer Elk River's bands, like the rest of the Sioux, fought their ancient enemies the Crows. Many small war parties went out from camp, twenty or thirty warriors in each group. Because of his growing reputation, Fox Dancer was selected to lead one small band, including Goosey, Little Man, Scraper, and other brave fighters. Lightning Man, hand healed but fingers still twisted awry, went with another band. It was just as well because the cousins were not on the best of terms.

Proud of his first command, Fox Dancer made a promise to The Great One Above to bring back more Crow horses than anyone. Carrying his ribboned lance, he watched his braves assemble. They were a fine sight, all dressed in new shirts of mountain-sheep or deerskin, decorated with tufts of dyed hair, bright pebbles and shells, scraps of bright calico. Long fringes trailed from sleeves to leggings, and faces were freshly painted with ocher and vermilion. Fox Dancer himself had his cheeks and forehead painted with small white spots, signifying a brave deed done in a snowstorm.

Although on the trail they would be covered, buffalo-skin shields now displayed sacred devices. Sun shone on the dull metal of the guns they had taken from the surveying party at The Battle of the Willows. Most of the Oglalas now had at least some kind of firearm, but Fox Dancer insisted on carrying no weapons but lance and hatchet. If he could not come close enough to count coup with those, he thought it unworthy to kill from a distance.

"Ready?" he called, his pony skittering and prancing. Feeling the excitement, the rest of the ponies started to caper too, and had to be restrained. They were the best of their owners' mounts; small, wiry, deer-legged horses with slanting quarters, hocks like mules', hides blotched and flared in patterns of brown and white and black. Pintos were prized; if a man had a horse all of one color, he would paint it first in spots and patches before riding it. One-color horses were bad luck.

"*Hopo!*" Fox Dancer shouted, raising his arm. "Let's go!"

As they left the camp, riding in single file toward the northern pass and Crow country, Fox Dancer saw Shell digging bear roots in the meadow. Ordinarily the women went out together for such homely tasks, and it was an occasion for fun and gossip. But Shell was alone. When he waved to her, she either did not see him or did not want to return his greeting.

That summer, things were not the same as previous years. The weather turned bad, with frequent and furious thunderstorms. Often they rode wet and miserable, shivering in the cold, ponies spattered with mud and war-paint streaked and faded. There was a lot of sneezing and coughing. Game was scarce, so they had to eat parched corn and moldy beans from their

war-bags, supplemented with a meager diet of roots and berries
gathered along the way. Meat had always been their principal
sustenance; without fresh meat they felt weak and listless.

The reason for the scarcity of game was not hard to understand. A lot of Hat People were in ancestral lands, areas that
had been from as long back as anyone remembered Sioux burial
grounds, not entered by themselves except to bring the honored
dead. Now, from afar, they saw large parties of Hat People
digging holes in the ground, damming streams, cutting down
trees to make queer long boxes and timber structures by the
creeks and rivers.

"What are they doing?" Scraper wanted to know. They sat
their bedraggled ponies on a high bluff, hidden behind a screen
of cottonwoods, watching the activity.

"I don't know," Fox Dancer admitted.

They watched the scurrying Hat People, swarming the clay
banks of the river like ants. To their ears came the distant
sound of axes, an insistent chorus of chopping.

Goosey wanted to fire a shot from his old musket at the in-
terlopers to show his disapproval, but Fox Dancer shook his
head. "There are too many of them," he pointed out. "Look!"
He held up both hands several times, snapping his fingers. "That
many, and more in the forest! What good is it to shoot one or
two? It will make them mad, and not do us any good. No, let
us just watch for a while, learn what we can, and then go look
for some Crows."

There was general grumbling; many of the band were not
happy with so young a leader. But finally they rode away from
the river, northwest into Crow country, anticipating the first
good fight of the season.

But everywhere they went, it seemed there were more of the
annoying Hat People. Work parties, heavily guarded by soldiers,
were making maps of Oglala land, their land. Over a hundred
white men, using queer, bucketlike, wheeled things drawn by
mules, cleared a roadway through a wooded area. Felled trees
lay in all directions, like matches spilled carelessly from a box.

Buffalo hunters, too, ranged their sacred lands, killing bulls, cows, young heifers, even the newly born.

From infancy the Oglalas ate buffalo meat. It was a gift from the Sioux gods; they reciprocated by taking only what they needed, and that only after elaborate ritual. They killed only mature animals, and before killing a buffalo it was proper to recite a little speech. "I need you. Please go into my lodge. If you do, I will give you red paint." Then, the animal slain, the hunter daubed the head with paint in gratitude. But there had been no ritual here, only senseless and greedy slaughter.

Fox Dancer swung off his pony, looking at a scene of recent carnage. Within a circle an arrow's flight in diameter lay over a hundred carcasses, probably killed by a man with a repeating Spencer rifle, the one the Oglalas said was loaded in the morning and shot all day. Flies buzzed thick on putrid carcasses, and the smell sickened. Most had been skinned for the hides, meat left to rot. Animals whose hides were not prime had simply had tongues cut out or hump steak hacked away for a hunter's supper.

"They were here last night," Scraper growled. "Those white men are not far away!"

Fox Dancer looked at the smoldering coals, the makeshift grill of twigs with remnants of scorched flesh. Buffalo was one of the Sioux gods. Buffalo looked after virgins and old people, and was on a par with the sun in ceremonies of the Medicine Lodge. Also, he was the patron of generosity, fecundity, industry, and ceremonies. Until now, the activities of the Hat People had been annoying and troublesome. But killing all the buffalo was different. The slaughter of the buffalo struck at their own sacred medicine, challenged the Sioux gods. Something would have to be done.

Goosey examined crushed tufts of grass, droppings from horses, a thrown-away tobacco bag. "They were here when the sun rose," he said. "We can catch them if we hurry!"

Again Fox Dancer shook his head. They were all very angry with him.

"Are you a coward?" Little Man demanded. "Blue Horse is a

scalp-shirt man! He would be ashamed if he knew his brother's son was afraid of a white man!"

Wearily Fox Dancer shook his head. "It is like trying to put smoke in a bag," he said. "Those hunters. They are on fast horses. They see us come, and they run away with their wagons and hides and things. Besides, there are too many of them. If we kill some, the rest will beg the One-Arm Colonel for more soldiers, and it will just get worse. No!" He touched his temple with a forefinger. "We have to think! That is what we have to do! Everybody remember what we have seen. Everyone think about it. Then later we can do something that important, not just shoot one or two people."

Anxious for a blooding, there was near mutiny. But Fox Dancer finally prevailed and they trotted on, still grumbling. I have to do something, Fox Dancer thought. We have not seen any Crows yet, and they want a good fight.

In Crow country at last, where they should have been well beyond the point where the Hat People penetrated, there were still evidences of their presence. Even the warlike Crows had been pushed farther and farther into their own country by the Hat People. Maybe the Crows are mad too, Fox Dancer thought. It was a wild, almost sacrilegious thought. But suppose the Crows and the Oglalas were to ally themselves against the common enemy? Suppose the Great Horse-Stealers and the Sioux banded together, put their considerable numbers across the path of the Hat People, forbade further encroachment by soldiers, miners, hunters, the fire wagons? *Suppose. Just suppose.* But he dared not mention it. In their rebellious mood, his command would probably kill him, even if Blue Horse was his uncle. They would kill him, and when they got back to camp explain how he had gone crazy, and they had had to destroy him.

On their way they came to a green valley, hemmed in by hills, with a stream of clear water lacing back and forth through it. The Oglalas knew this valley; it was a favorite place to stop and rest. But this time there was something new. Running along the bottoms, sometimes following the stream, sometimes crossing it, a shiny wire was suspended from freshly peeled poles. The

wire sparkled in the sun, red glints glanced from it. *Copper.*
The Oglalas knew copper. It could be twisted, hammered, rolled
into rich and subtle ornaments. Goosey ran forward and grasped
one of the poles, pulling it this way and that, trying to uproot
it. But Fox Dancer flung himself off his pinto, grabbing Goosey
and wrestling him away.

"No!" he cried. "Wait!"

Goosey's slack lips dropped open. "What? What do you say?"

"That thing." Fox Dancer pointed to the slender thread of
the wire. "That is a thing the white man talks over."

There was silence. Goosey started to laugh, thinking it a joke.
But Fox Dancer went on.

"I know what I am saying. The white men talk over that
wire. They talk a long way, they talk over mountains and across
rivers. The red-hair man told me. At the fort I saw the soldiers
talking over the wire, with a little shiny thing that went clack-
clack."

Little Man pushed forward. "Well, that is a good reason to
cut it down, then!"

"No," Fox Dancer insisted. "I have a plan."

It would not do much injury to the white men, perhaps, but
it was something. Duffy had spoken of the talking wire, the
way the shiny metal carried strange clicking messages that
warned the walk-a-heaps of prowling Sioux war parties. Metal,
Fox Dancer understood, could carry words; string could not.
But what about—well, grapevines, for instance? While they
watched he climbed the hill to the edge of the trees and found
a stand of wild grapes. With his knife he cut a long runner,
bringing it back to the waiting group.

"Now," he ordered, "pull out the pole. Be careful not to
break the wire!"

They obeyed, digging carefully around the base of the pole
with knives and hatchets, carefully lowering the pole. The shiny
wire tightened, but did not break.

Fox Dancer cut the wire with his knife, severing a section
the length of his two arms spread wide apart, and tossed the
cut-out section to Goosey, who snatched it up and wound it in

a gleaming coil around his upper arm. "What are you doing now?" Scraper asked.

Carefully Fox Dancer bridged the cut-out gap with the grapevine. It did not look much like copper wire, but hoisted into place the break would be hard to detect. It might take the Hat People a long time to find.

"There!" he said in satisfaction. "Now they cannot talk anymore. Raise the pole. And when you put dirt back, scatter leaves and grass around so no one can see what we have done."

Excited and laughing, they erected the pole and looked at their handiwork.

"That is very good," Little Man approved. "Friend, maybe you are *Iktomi*, yourself, the trickster!"

In high spirits they rode down the valley, and almost immediately ran into a small party of Crows. The fight was short and furious, spilling back and forth, up the sides of the narrow valley, splashing through the shallows of the stream. There was a lot of gunfire and excitement, plenty of opportunity to count coup. They captured a string of ponies the Crows had been leading, and some panniers of supplies that included white men's tobacco and looking glasses. But Walking Bull was shot through the chest with a Crow arrow, and died soon after.

Well, it was one of the things that happened. And Walking Bull had had a good time in the fight. Goosey took off his new copper bracelet and wound it around the dead man's arm before they buried him. For the occasion they all put on their best clothes. They built a platform high in the trees bordering the valley, and put the body up there, wrapped in the red blanket. At the foot of the tree they stuck a pole in the earth and tied Walking Bull's drum, his sashes, and his rattle to it. Afterward, they painted their faces white in mourning. The next morning they ran into another band of Crows, this one larger, but were forced to flee into the hills to escape. It had been a good fight, too, though they lost some of the newly captured horses back to the Crows.

"Did you see me?" Little Man shouted, slapping himself on his bare chest. "I rode up to that ugly man on the horse with the bad eye and hit him with my lance! I could have stuck him right through his big belly, but I just beat him over the shoulders with the handle, and broke it, too!" Proudly he showed them the splintered butt of the lance. It was a great coup, one of the bravest things a man could do—ride up to a foe and strike him, and get away again. It was a braver deed than to just kill someone, meaning as it did utter contempt for an adversary.

"But did you see *me*?" Goosey demanded. He held out a dripping knife. "I took this away from a man and stabbed him with it! His own knife! He was surprised, I can tell you! He just looked at me, and then fell down!" Goosey raced his pony back and forth, whooping and yelling in delight.

It looked like it might be a good summer after all, and they forgot—almost forgot—the intrusions of the white men, the slaughtered buffalo, the talking wire. It was like old times, the times before there were any Hat People, only themselves, although Fox Dancer seemed preoccupied, and did not laugh much, or talk.

On and on they went, heading northwest. Days passed, weeks passed. There were a lot of fights, the sun shone, they took a lot of Crow horses and lost a few of their own. Two more of the party were killed in fights, but they buried them, too, and rode on. The summer waned; soon it would be time to go back to Elk River's camp in the mountains, to show their booty, to speak of victories, to tell some of the women their men were dead. Fox Dancer thought often of Shell, she of the sleek, dark braids and gentle eyes, the soft way of talking, almost like a child. An ache came in his loins. He had known that feeling before, many times before. Now, with the long absence from camp, he felt it warm and powerful and demanding. But there was nothing he could do about it; other important things came first.

In the last fight of the summer they galloped through a small Crow village on the slopes below the Big Horn Mountains and drove everybody away. It was a rich haul; many horses, even a lot of corn and dried meat and things they did not have enough pack animals to carry off. They set fire to the Crow lodges and watched as the village burned. But from among the flaming lodges an old man scuttled, hair and clothing on fire. He had hidden there, only to be driven out by the flames. Little Man raised his gun to shoot but Fox Dancer knocked up Little Man's arm and ran to the fleeing elder, rolling him on the ground till he put out the flames.

"Old man," he said. "I want to talk to you."

Fearful, the elder looked at him. Face and hands were smudged and grimy, most of his hair burned away, and jewels of sparks stitched through his hide shirt and leggings. In a croaking voice he asked, "What do you want? Kill me, why don't you?" and spat at them.

The rest of his band gathered around Fox Dancer, curious. Spare a Crow?

"Old man," he said. "I will not kill you. I want you to take a message to the chiefs of your people. I want you to tell them something for me."

Goosey was impatient. "We had better kill him and go away," he protested. He gestured with his rifle toward the hillside. "The Crows have gone up there. In a minute they will get their people together and come back down on us!"

Fox Dancer shook his head. "Wait." To the old man he said, "I am Fox Dancer, nephew of Blue Horse, of the Oglalas. Elk River is our chief. Even the Crows know about Elk River."

"Yes," the old man admitted, trying to rub glowing sparks out of his shirt. "I know of Elk River."

"There are a lot of Hat People coming here now," Fox Dancer went on. "They are everywhere—on the plains, in the mountains, in the grass, on the rivers, among the trees. They dig for gold, they plow up our land, they string talking wires, they kill the buffalo. So maybe it is better if we—the Crows and the Sioux—fight the white men, instead of each other."

The old man looked startled. Mouth dropped open, ancient skin wrinkled into networks of perplexity. "What did you say?"

Fox Dancer's band crowded around, incredulous. "What did he say? Not fight the Crows? Did he say that? Did Fox Dancer say that?"

"But it has always been this way!" the old man cried, indignant. "We have always fought the Sioux! And they fight us! How else would it be?"

Little Man agreed. "This is silly talk, friend!" he shouted. "What is the use of hanging around here, talking crazy talk! And anyway, up there"—he pointed toward the hill with his lance—"they are getting together again. Listen!"

It was true. From the cover of the trees they could hear voices, shouted commands, stamping and whinnying of horses.

Fox Dancer gripped the old man by the shoulder. "Listen," he commanded, "listen to me! Someday there will be more Hat People than Oglalas. More white men than all the rest of the Sioux—the Miniconjou, the Brulé, the Hunkpapa—all the rest of them. Someday there will be more Hat People than all of us put together, the Sioux and the Crows and the Rees and the Crees and everybody. So maybe we better get together and fight them. That is the only way we can push them out of our country —get together, fight the white men like we were one people."

The old man looked bewildered.

"Remember what I say!" Fox Dancer shouted. He pushed the man from him so that he tumbled in a pile of smoking rags, and jumped on his horse. "Remember what I say, and tell your people!"

His action caused consternation. All the way back to Elk River's camp there was heated discussion. Not fight the Crows! A man might as well tell the sun not to come up in the morning! It had been done this way always, ever since there were Sioux and Crows on the face of the earth! Rock said it should be that way, and there would be trouble with the gods if anyone tried to change it. But Fox Dancer would not enter into any of the talk. "I have said what I have said," he told them, and rode silently on, not looking to right or left.

When they got back to the camp, summer was nearly gone. Already the nights were growing cold. The geese took longer and longer flights each day, eating a lot of wild rice against the long journey south. Riding in, the war party saw signs of trouble.

The women were crying, and some had gashed their arms and legs in grief; the men smeared ashes on their faces. Elk River had died while Fox Dancer and his band were gone, and some of the women had stoned Shell and driven her away from the camp. *Wit-ko-win,* they said. *Whore!*

# CHAPTER SEVEN

Tearfully, Twin Woman gave Fox Dancer all the news. Since he had no woman, she cooked for him and kept his lodge clean. As she stirred the stew and boiled coffee she told him what had happened.

"Anyone could see the poor girl was going to have a baby. Oh, maybe the men didn't see it, but women know such things. Everybody thought it was Lightning Man's child—that he had slept with her because it was taking him so long to get all the presents Elk River wanted for his daughter. But when Lightning Man came back from fighting the Crows, he was mad. He said it was not his child, that it belonged to that red-hair man, the one called"— she looked at Fox Dancer, drying her eyes—"Duf-Duf—"

"Duffy!" he said, impatient. "But where is she now? Where has she gone?"

Sniffling, the old woman rambled on at her own pace.

"Lightning Man and Bear Tooth went to our father Elk River and spoke against Shell. They said her baby belonged to Duffy, that it would bring bad luck to the camp, bad luck to the Oglalas, to all the Sioux. Elk River did not know what to do. After all, it was his own daughter! But he had seen her going about with the red-hair man, and there had been a lot of talk. So he covered his face, and let them drive her out. The women threw stones, and Shell ran into the trees. After that, Elk River would not eat or drink or do anything. He just kept his face covered. After a while he died. That is what happened." She gestured with her thumb in the symbol for *truth*.

Angry, Fox Dancer grabbed the stew spoon away from her

and threw it into a corner of the *tipi*. "When did this happen? How long ago did Shell run away?"

Frightened, she stared at him. "Three days. Maybe four. I don't remember!" Beginning to weep again, she rubbed her arm where he had grasped her. "I am sorry about it. I did not throw any stones. It was wrong. But there is no need for you to hurt an old woman who is telling you the truth!"

It was dusk, an autumn dusk, trees dark with a purplish haze and first stars beginning to prick the night. He ran into the woods, calling her name.

"Shell! Shell!"

Under his feet something stirred, and then rustled away in the silence following his call.

"Shell! Where are you?"

A nightbird made a flutelike sound, and he heard the soft beat of wings over his head; a shadowy figure drifted into the twilight. The forest smelled of coming winter; wet, dead leaves, stagnant water, black earth. *Three days. Maybe four.* She could have wandered a long way. Even now she might be dead, dead from hunger and thirst and exposure. Or perhaps dead only from grief. Grief had killed Elk River.

"Shell!" he called. "Do you hear me?"

It was dark among the trees and he blundered about, falling and cutting his knee, rising, then falling again into a pool on his hands and knees. Rising from the muck, he heard a chorus of chugging grunts, and eyes stared at him from the black water. Now there was a little moon, a yellow crust that gave small light. Wiping muddy hands on his shirt, he staggered on, calling her name.

After a while, panting and exhausted, he leaned against a tree. This was foolish; how could a man find someone in the trees, at night, especially someone who might not want to be found? Shell's shame was great. Even now she might be cowering under a bush, hearing his call but not daring to answer. The thought made him frantic.

"Shell!" he cried. A mocking echo drifted back to him through the trees. "I am looking for you! I will take care of you! Only tell me where you are!"

For a moment he thought it was another owl, a white owl soaring silently among the branches, drifting through a moonlit open space, passing behind a tree and then emerging again, nearer this time.

*Father Owl.* He half thought, half spoke the words. *Have you seen her?* He knew she was dead. *Where is she lying? I will go to her and wrap her in a new blanket. I will put a willow garland on her head, and burn white sage at her feet.*

But it was not an owl. It was instead a pale, frightened face.

"Shell?" he called. Then, "Shell!"

Weeping, she ran to his arms and clung like a child frightened by tales of *Mistai*, the whistling ghost who walks about by night and scares children by scratching on the lodge skins near their heads.

"Are you well?" he asked, trying to look at her. But she clung to him so tightly it was impossible.

"Can you walk, then?"

Stifling sobs, she nodded. But when he turned to accompany her back to his lodge, the slender legs collapsed. He picked her up and carried her across the moonlit meadow.

All the people had gone to sleep. The lodges were silver tapers in the moonlight. In the corrals horses stirred as he approached, and a late-wandering dog sniffed at his heels and then padded into the meadow after rabbits.

Twin Woman had gone home to Man-Who-Never-Walked. Fox Dancer's fire was only glowing coals, and he laid Shell on the buffalo robes and set about rekindling the fire. She watched him, silent. After a while she said, "I hoped you would come. I knew you would come." Her voice caught, and she turned her face to the wall. "You were the only one that would help me."

Kneeling beside her, uncomfortable at doing such woman's work, he fed her the rest of the stew. She ate ravenously, and then, ashamed of her appetite, said, "I was a long time hiding out there. I drank water from dirty pools, but there was nothing to eat except berries and a few wild plums." She tried to get up, then, saying, "I must not stay here! What will people think of you? A woman like me, in your lodge! In Fox Dancer's lodge!"

Gently he pushed her back. "Rest. We will talk later of what must be done."

She was stronger than he thought. Three days—four—of hunger and privation had not weakened her very much.

"No!" she said, pushing away his hand. "I—I am rested now, and fed."

"But where will you go?"

She was silent. All he could see was the white parting in her black braids, firelight shining on sleek, smooth braids. The musky scent rose to his nostrils, and he put out a hand, fascinated, to touch them. This was part of what he felt so much of late; part of the land and the sky and the bursting feeling in his heart.

"I don't know." For a moment he thought she was going to cry, but she didn't. Instead, she only kept her head bowed, avoiding his eyes. There was something tense and expectant in the way she sat, head bowed, waiting.

"We will go against them," he told her. "We will go against Lightning Man and Bear Tooth. Bear Tooth has magic, yes; he has his yellowhammer bird, and he knows how to make spells and brew charms and things like that. But I have strong medicine, too." He went on and on, rambling, trying to comfort her, his mind elsewhere. The smooth, luminous streak through her dark hair—straight and clean as an arrow's flight. He touched it, and felt her tremble under his fingers.

"Lightning Man," he said. "I do not fear Lightning Man. You and I—we—we will—"

He was feeling very strange. His own voice sounded odd and faraway. Her hair came to seem like waves in a midnight pond, the wind gently stroking them into small ripples that caught the moon. But it was his own hand stroking the dark locks. He felt her press softly against him, the pressure of breast and thigh against his own.

Together, locked in an embrace, they slipped down on the heavy-furred robe, Shell all the time yielding yet somehow pulling away, one hand about his neck and the other trapped between his chest and her own, pushing.

"No," she objected, very softly, almost as if she did not want him to hear. "No. Please."

Long days on the trail had made him hungry. He raised himself on an elbow and looked down into her eyes. They were deep but somehow without meaning; dark mirrors that reflected only what was outside, not within.

"No," she said again.

Caught up with passion, he pulled aside her dress. At first it did not come. Impatiently he pulled again. The sinew stitching came away, and Shell lay naked. Her body shimmered palely in the firelight; breasts high and jutting, narrow waist, a full and fecund swell of the hips, legs slender and supple. She did not speak, only looked at him with that curious, flat gaze.

"I see," Fox Dancer said. He took a deep breath.

"Yes." It was not so much a word as a release of breath, a breath long held in fear and shame.

She had wound the elaborately knotted cord about her waist, tightly between her legs, around her thighs. It was the ritual cord Sioux women wore when their men were away on the hunt, or on the warpath. No man other than her husband could remove that cord; it was sacred.

"Duffy," Fox Dancer murmured.

"Yes."

He helped her fold the torn dress about her and sat for a long time, squatting, looking into the fire. It was going out. It would need more wood soon.

She touched his hand and began to cry. "Why did you not leave me there in the woods? Why did you not leave me there to die? I never wanted to hurt anyone!"

Silent, he let her cry it out, and stared into the fire as if it held a secret. After a while—it must have been almost dawn—she slept, catching her breath from time to time in a little sob. The fire went out; Fox Dancer made no move to restore it. The red-hair man, the fox man, was still, in a way, with the Oglalas.

Near or far, for better or for worse, Lew Duffy was a presence
among them.

↔

Blue Horse had been chosen as the new chief of the Oglalas.
He was a brave and good man, respected by everybody. Now,
aware of the dissension about Shell, he called a council meeting
to settle matters. In the big lodge he sat on a dais covered with
furs and blankets, carrying Elk River's pipe as his badge of
office. The pipe was intricately carved, both the cherrywood
stem and the bowl of soapstone, and ornamented with duck
feathers, signifying endurance and patience, because the feathers of the duck turn away water and wind. Around his neck
Blue Horse wore on a thong the chief's whistle, made of the
legbone of an eagle, and his face was painted with diagonal
stripes of yellow and red and white.

Lightning Man was there, too, as the plaintiff, accompanied
by Bear Tooth, the shaman. Lightning Man now wore fresh-
painted wound marks on his body, one straight, horizontal,
dripping-red line that meant an arrow wound, and a painted
red disk that signified a bullet wound. Fresh scalps were sewn
to his shirt; he had had a good summer against the Crows.

The shaman was impressive also. He wore a band of black
fur around his head, and a buffalo horn attached to each ear.
Over his shoulders was thrown the shaman's coat, fur-side out,
as no common man was permitted to wear it, and his face was
painted blue, with a white moon on his forehead and a star
across the bridge of his nose. Both of them stared hard-eyed at
Fox Dancer, and spoke in low tones to each other.

Because of the importance of the meeting the Bad Faces
and the Midnight Strong Hearts were attending. These were
powerful secret societies; from their ranks the chiefs seemed
generally to be selected. Blue Horse had been Drum-Keeper of
the Midnight Strong Hearts for a long time.

Fox Dancer sat near the door, the hide case with the Hat
People's transit between his legs. On the trail that summer he
worried about leaving it behind, but did not want to take the
chance that some lucky Crow would capture it and the possible

magic along with it. His worry was, however, well-founded on other grounds. Bear Tooth, Twin Woman told him, had sniffed around his *tipi* while he was gone. She thought the shaman was trying to steal the transit. Fearing the medicine man, the old woman hid the instrument under her bed of woven-willow mats to keep it safe.

Lightning Man was greatly upset at what his cousin had done, but made an effort to control himself. At his father's gesture, he got up and told the story of Shell; how the *wit-ko-win* refused him, to whom Elk River had promised her; how she shamelessly lay with the red-hair man Duffy; how her growing belly gave her away and killed her father Elk River with shame.

"I was very sad," Lightning Man said, making the sign: *heart laid on the ground.* "I wanted her for my wife, but she was faithless. A lot of the women knew she was a whore, so they stoned her and drove her out of the camp."

There was a murmur of sympathy. Everyone knew Lightning Man had worked hard and long to get enough horses and things to pay Elk River for his bride.

"Now," Lightning Man complained, "someone has gone against the gods. Someone went out and brought this *wit-ko-win* back to camp!" Angrily he pointed to Fox Dancer. "That is the man! That is the troublemaker! He always thinks he is better and smarter than anyone else! But this time he has gone against the gods, and ought to be punished!"

Blue Horse gestured to his nephew with the handle of an eagle-feather fan. "What do you say to this?"

"He is a foolish man!" Fox Dancer protested. He was angry, but fought to keep his voice and gestures under control. "Shell is no *wit-ko-win*! She is faithful to her man, I tell you. She always has been!"

"The red-hair man!" his cousin shouted. "Oh, yes, that red-hair man! She was faithful to him, she was his woman! Shell lay with him when she was promised to me!"

"The red-hair man," Fox Dancer admitted. "Yes, the man called Duffy. Shell was a foolish girl, maybe. But many girls are foolish. And when they grow up to be women, they can be foolish too. A man knows that. A man makes allowances for that. And maybe we were all foolish, in a way."

Blue Horse leaned forward, frowning. "We are all foolish?" He was annoyed; possibly his bad stomach hurt him.

"Excuse me, Uncle." Fox Dancer was apologetic. "But the man called Duffy sang funny songs. The children liked him, and followed him about. He was a brave man, and the people began to like him. They would let him come into their lodges and drink coffee and tell them stories. Shell was foolish, like the rest of us. She listened to Duffy's stories. Women are not very smart, so he talked soft to her and got her to share his blanket. That is how it happened."

He had a feeling the tide was changing. For a long time he had known he was a persuasive talker, and now began to have a feeing of power, of growing confidence and ease. Lightning Man and Bear Tooth must have felt it too, because they looked uneasy and muttered a great deal to each other.

"The gods say 'drive out a *wit-ko-win.*' All right. But Shell is not a whore. She is only a misguided girl. And she is the child of an honored old man, of Elk River, who did not know what to do when these two—" He pointed at Lightning Man and Bear Tooth. "When these two evil men came carrying tales about his daughter! *They* are the two who should be stoned! They are the ones who should be driven out!"

Lightning Man sprang up, face contorted, and ran at Fox Dancer. The doorkeeper sprang between them, and Lightning Man shook his fist, breathing hard. "You will pay for this, cousin! Shame! I do not have to take insults like that from anyone!"

Lightning Man's behavior brought a murmur of disapproval from the secret societies. This was an important meeting; dignity had to be preserved. Blue Horse took a long pull at the soapstone pipe, waiting for wisdom and calm to come to everybody. Finally most were quiet, though some still murmured behind cupped hands. One of the Midnight Strong Hearts looked at Fox Dancer, then nodded; only a slight inclination of his head, but did it indicate approval?

From somewhere came a flutelike, whistling sound. Bear Tooth cocked an ear at his stuffed yellowhammer, and reported, "This bird is trying to say something to us. We should all listen."

The council lodge was quiet. From the west came a distant rolling of thunder as an early storm formed over the mountains. A child playing in the meadow laughed; a woman was chopping wood to cook the evening meal. Bear Tooth, squatting among his charms and amulets, his painted sacred buffalo skull and his bundles of selected magic grasses, closed his eyes and swayed to and fro, listening to the yellowhammer. The flutelike singing continued, though the shaman's lips were tightly closed. After a while Bear Tooth nodded, as if satisfied, and opened his eyes.

"This bird flies a long way. Once it flew all the way to the country of our enemies the Crows." He appeared to listen again to the bird, and then continued. "This bird tells me a very strange thing. It says that Fox Dancer is a bad man. This bird saw him go to a Crow village and say the Oglalas and the Crows should be friends."

There was a stir, uneasy movement. Crows? Friends?

"This bird flew over the Crow camp, and heard Fox Dancer say those very words. Imagine that! Oglalas to be friends of the Crows! This bird was so surprised he flew right back and told me everything." Bear Tooth got to his feet and pointed at Fox Dancer. His painted face was wet with sweat; talking with the bird, he claimed, was a great strain on him.

"Why would a man talk like that?" he demanded. "What is Fox Dancer trying to do—betray us to the Crows, the *Absaroka*, the horse stealers?"

Pandemonium broke out. Even the dignified warriors of the secret societies were alarmed. The Crows were their hereditary enemies. Summer campaigns against them were Oglala history, going back in the Winter Calendar as far as anyone could remember. Treating with the Crows was more than treason; it was blasphemy!

"Is this true?" Blue Horse demanded, glowering at Fox Dancer. "Is it true, what this sacred bird says?"

The yellowhammer was feared and respected by the Oglalas. It was their collective medicine, and Fox Dancer felt his throat tighten, heart beat faster. He would have to think fast, talk fast, not only for Shell and her unborn baby, but for himself.

"It is true," he admitted, "but that bird did not tell everything. It did not see everything. There is more—much more."

Deliberately he got to his feet, unfastening the thongs that bound the Hat People's three-legged god into its leather case. Forcing himself to be calm, he worked at a difficult knot. His fingers trembled, but at last he freed the thong.

"There are sacred birds," he said, propping the instrument on its three legs and freeing the brass things that restrained the needle of the compass and the polished barrel of the telescope. "There are sacred bones, too. There are sacred skulls, and sacred songs, and sacred dances. There are a lot of sacred things."

They watched him, intent. Blue Horse frowned and sucked at his pipe, smoke wreathing his face. From the upper recesses of the lodge a fat spider swung down on a strand of silk, and as it passed the doorway the afternoon sun caught the thread and it shone with luminous fire.

"This is a sacred thing, too," Fox Dancer went on. "It is sacred to the Hat People. The white men have strong magic, and it took me a long time to learn how to use their medicine. This thing is very dangerous. A man has to be strong and brave even to come near a dangerous thing like this three-legged god here."

Goosey, sitting near, drew back in alarm, looking uneasily at the transit. Little Man made a ritual sign to protect himself, and one of the Midnight Strong Hearts muttered a charm against evil.

"I look through here," Fox Dancer announced, kneeling before the instrument, "and I have learned to see a long way into the times to come." He put his eye to the telescope. "A man that is not afraid can see secret things in here, things that have not even happened yet. That is how I saw that we must all come together to fight the Hat People, even the Crows and the Shoshones. We must all come together and fight, because soon the white men will come out here in their fire wagons and try to hurt us, to drive us away, to take Oglala land for themselves."

The Oglalas did not understand the concept of allies. A man fought to count coup, to do brave deeds, to ride up to an enemy —a Crow or Shoshone—and strike him with a lance, a bow, or even a switch. If a man could do that, and get away unscathed, it was the bravest of deeds. So who needed allies? If there were more of the enemy, it meant only the more chance to count coup!

Bear Tooth, very angry, waved the stuffed bird and yelled, "Do not believe him! That is all lies! There is nothing sacred about that thing! Fox Dancer is a fool!"

It was one strong medicine against another. Uncertain, people looked at each other. Some scratched their heads with their carved sticks, others rubbed their chins. Never, for as long as anyone could remember, had there been a real challenge to the yellowhammer. But Fox Dancer sounded reasonable. Besides, it was well known that the young man was a powerful and gifted dreamer himself, always thinking, always trying to figure things out. Though he was young, what he said could not readily be discounted.

"What this thing shows me is that the Oglalas are in danger," Fox Dancer said, tapping the telescope. "It shows me we need help even from the Crows and Shoshones. That is why I spoke to the Crows, told them they must join us, and other people, too." When Bear Tooth protested, waving his rattle and starting a medicine chant, Fox Dancer went on, speaking even louder, almost shouting.

"There is more medicine in this thing." He tapped the compass. "This little arrow here always points to the truth. I found that out. Now I am going to tell you something."

Blue Horse gestured to Bear Tooth to be silent. The shaman sat down, fondling the stuffed bird and glowering.

"While I was gone on the fight against the Crows," Fox Dancer told them, "a bad man tried to steal this three-legged medicine. He was an Oglala man, a man who always had strong medicine but who is getting old and foolish. His medicine has lost all its strength. So he tried to find this thing where it was hidden, and steal it." He bent over the tripod, pointing. "This little arrow speaks to me. This arrow always points to the truth. So—who is this bad man? Who is the thief? Who is the foolish and evil man who has no good medicine anymore, and tries to steal some?"

Fox Dancer motioned to Goosey. Reluctantly, Goosey knelt over the compass and followed its direction; past Little Man, past Blue Horse, past the secret societies. Following the course of the arrow, Goosey stared at Bear Tooth, who was standing defiantly against the far wall of the lodge.

"Who is it?" Blue Horse demanded.

Goosey pointed. "Him. Bear Tooth."

"It is a lie!" the shaman shouted. "It is all a trick! That thing does not show the truth!"

But others crowded forward. They looked along the arrow at Bear Tooth, and began to mutter among themselves. Stealing another man's medicine was a serious business, and could be punished by banishment. Besides, this looked like more powerful medicine than the stuffed bird.

"He is lying!" Lightning Man protested. "Don't listen to him! It is all a trick!"

"No," Fox Dancer said. "It is not a trick." Squatting before the transit, he trained the telescope in the direction of the arrow and adjusted it on the angry face of Bear Tooth.

"I can see what is going to happen," he cried. "I can see Rock and Thunder and Sun and Buffalo and all the Oglala gods punishing Bear Tooth because he tried to steal medicine! Everyone knows the gods give us our medicine. They give it to good men to use, and it is evil to try to steal medicine from anybody. So in this little looking thing I see Bear Tooth running away from camp. I see him falling down, and getting up and running again! I see him—"

"Stop!" Bear Tooth waved the yellowhammer in a desperate incantation. "This is foolishness you are talking! My bird—my sacred bird—"

"I see him," Fox Dancer went inexorably on, his voice rising to a strong, resonant chant. "I see him running away, running into the trees, into the mountains, with the angry gods beating him with switches. They drive him into the high mountains, where ghosts and evil spirits—*sikisn, mohin*—grab him and pull him down into a big hole in the ground and eat him!"

For one horrible moment Bear Tooth stared at the probing glass eye. His whole body trembled. Sweat sparkled on his painted face, a string of spittle ran from a corner of his mouth. He swayed, and for a moment looked as if he would fall in a faint. Then, suddenly, he sprang into the air and dashed from the ceremonial *tipi*. He ran into the hides bordering the door and tore some loose. Off balance, he tottered for a moment, then ran out the door, yelling and screaming strange words no one remembered ever having heard. They were simply not in the Oglala language.

But Bear Tooth did run away from greater magic, that was a fact. Pursued by the truth-seeking arrow, followed by the deadly glass eye, he ran into the woods and toward the mountains, jumping in the air and screaming as the gods beat his legs with switches. He was eventually seized in the high mountains by *sikisn* and *mohin*, and eaten. He was never seen again, never came back; the stuffed bird never sang again.

# CHAPTER EIGHT

The Union Pacific continued its advance. Far to the east of the Oglalas, track-laying crews advanced the steel road at the rate of a mile a day, and the tracks stitched westward to meet the Central Pacific, building from San Francisco. The red men resisted; there were skirmishes between railroad workers and Indians. Eastern newspapers printed accounts of pitched battles. The Washington *Daily Chronicle* told of a railroad crew ambushed and losing most of its workers, survivors escaping on a hand car. *Harper's* published woodcuts showing in detail the horrible tortures inflicted by the Sioux on unlucky captives.

The Philadelphia *Press* greatly increased its circulation with a series of feature articles titled "A Chronology of Sioux Atrocities in The West." A particularly pathetic account told of a party of Indians who took up a rail on the Union Pacific and laid ties across the track to derail a work train. The engineer and stoker were killed. When the conductor and brakeman and railway workers jumped off, they were beset by howling savages. The brakeman was shot immediately, and fell. His tormentor dismounted and scalped him, then stripped the body of all clothing except shoes. The rest of the crew escaped into the bushes, and the Indians set fire to the cars.

Early the next morning, another train approaching was flagged down by a hideous-looking object which proved to be the brakeman. Though shot through the body and scalped, he had managed to walk a distance along the track to warn the train he knew would arrive in the morning. Later someone found a scalp, and when it was taken into the cars, it was immediately recognized by the wounded man as his own. The scalp was put into a bucket of medicated water to preserve it; later an effort was made by surgeons to sew it onto the man's head, hoping it would take root and grow again. But the surgery was unsuccessful. "Although the man lived," the telegraph story to the *Press* recounted, "he had a perfectly horrible-looking head. He said later that the bullet, while knocking him down, did not render him unconscious. His greatest trial in that terrible night was the necessity of shamming dead, not daring to cry out when the Indian was slowly sawing at his head-covering with a very dull knife."

In spite of these atrocities, however, there was in Washington and New York City a small but powerful organization which called itself The Friends of the Indian. They believed there was really no "Indian problem"; all that was necessary was to reason with the Indians—give them gifts to induce them to sign a treaty, then guarantee them their own inviolate lands (a sufficient distance removed from the Union Pacific right-of-way) and make of them peaceful farmers and good citizens. Even the Commissioner of Indian Affairs held to this philosophy, though it was bitterly opposed by the Army. The generals, seeing one war coming to an end, spoiled for another with the intransigent Sioux.

↔

In winter snows Shell's child was born, a curious, wizened infant with dark eyes and a ruff of flame-colored hair. She named him Sun Hair, and she and the baby formed Fox Dancer's household. Shell cooked for him, mended his clothes, sewed dyed quills on his shirt, performed all the wifely rites except one. Fox Dancer became an elder brother to her, and a kindly uncle to the child.

In those days, too, his stature among the Oglalas grew. There were among the Sioux many shamans, medicine men, sorcerers, and others with unnatural powers. Some could pick up burning coals in their fingers and not be harmed. Others had bullet-proof shirts. Some knew how to talk to birds and animals, and certain others could brew the juices of various plants into potions to restore a lost love or make impotent a rival. Fox Dancer was unique among all these; he had conquered a white man's god and made it his own. With the three-legged god he could spy out the truth, and by looking through the glass eye, see into the future. The Oglalas were proud of him. He was known among the rest of the Sioux—the Brulés, the Miniconjou, the Hunkpapa. Even the Crows and the Shoshones, it was said, knew of Fox Dancer and his medicine.

But he himself was not confident. Sitting in the firelighted *tipi*, peering through the darkened glass, he did indeed believe he saw patterns, shifting luminous beads of light, odd, snakelike creatures. This was part of the magic of the instrument, he felt sure. On the other hand, he did not know how to interpret what he saw. Too, the little arrow on top acted in baffling and mysterious ways. Guns it knew; it would follow a gunbarrel held close to it, but would not do so with a leaden musket ball. Sometimes it swung wildly and would not rest. It was all very confusing.

On the other hand, the three-legged god had helped him to save Shell and her baby, no doubt about that. The arrow pointed out Bear Tooth as a thief and an evil man, and the glass eye pursued him till he ran shrieking into the mountains. So there was powerful magic to it, after all. What he now had to do was pursue his study, and someday it would yield all its secrets. In the meantime he was greatly respected, often consulted by Blue Horse and the elders of the tribe. It was a good feeling, a heady feeling for a young man.

Lightning Man, however, still opposed his cousin. Shame rankled in him, shame engendered by his defeat in the matter of Shell. He had lost his principal support when Bear Tooth fled, but managed to gather around him a few malcontents who spread stories about Fox Dancer, stories that there was no magic at all to the transit, that it was not a god, merely a thing to look through, that Fox Dancer himself was a deceiver. In council, Lightning Man attacked Fox Dancer. After all, Lightning Man was the son of Blue Horse, and Blue Horse was now principal chief of the Oglalas. That fact alone gave the angry young man standing. He professed not to dislike Fox Dancer himself, but to be concerned only with principle.

"I do not hate this man," he explained. "Maybe he *has* some good medicine. Maybe he knows how to use that thing in a way I do not understand. But a man like me can have his own medicine. His own private medicine can speak truth to him even if he does not have any little arrow that goes round and round. So my medicine tells me that there is danger in that three-legged thing. Someday it will bring trouble to all of us. Someday my cousin will look into it and it will trick him, betray the Oglalas, bring hunger and fire and death."

However, there were few supporters. The Oglalas recognized Lightning Man's right to speak, they granted him bravery in fighting what he believed to be evil, but that was about all that happened.

Fox Dancer felt badly about the whole thing. He did not really want to fight with his cousin. He remembered when they were small boys and played the Hoop and Stick Game, or made buffalo-rib sleds to coast down snowy hills. Even then Lightning Man had a temper, but he was generous and brave, fun to be with. Now, with his obsession about the transit, he became moody and sullen. After a while Fox Dancer began to fear for Shell and her baby. He was afraid Lightning Man, in a fit of passion, might do them harm.

He did not want to worry Shell, however. On long winter nights he sat beside her and the baby, listening to her sing to Sun Hair, listening to the baby's contented gurgles. One night, seeing her stare for a long time into the fire, he asked, "You are thinking of him? You are thinking of Duffy?"

She turned a long gaze on him, then went back to rocking the baby. "Yes," she murmured, "I miss him. Sometimes I wake in the night, and wonder where he is, how far away he has gone from me—whether . . ." She turned her face away. "Whether I will ever see him again."

Others missed Duffy, too. Goosey recalled funny things Duffy said. Man-Who-Never-Walked talked about what a good student the red-hair man had been, learning quickly about the Oglalas and their history and ways. Twin Woman, whenever she cooked, would say, "That red-hair man should be here. He liked my stews." One day Fox Dancer, walking through the village, saw a little girl sitting on a stump in the snow, crooning to her stick doll "Rye whisky, rye whisky," she was singing, very softly. "If you do not give me rye whisky I surely will die." The child did not know the meaning of the words, but it was a lullaby for her doll, and a remembrance of the red-hair man.

When spring came the Oglalas went on their annual trading pilgrimage to Fort Jackson. Blue Horse, his stomach feeling better, led the party. When they got there, the Oglalas saw a great deal of excitement and activity. A lot of other Sioux were there; Miniconjous, Brulés, Two Kettles, Sans-Arcs. Lodges surrounded the fort, pennoned lances whipped in the wind, children played and dogs barked. Forsythe, the One-Arm Colonel, called them all together for a big meeting. There was rum, and plenty of calico cloth and beads and Lone Jack for presents.

"Because," the colonel said through his interpreter, "I have a message for the Sioux, a message that comes all the way from our new President in Washington, the Great White Father, over the talking wire. Our old chief—the one called Abraham Lincoln —is dead. A wicked man killed him. Now President Johnson is the new chief, and he wants to talk to the Sioux."

Puzzled, the Miniconjous and Sans-Arcs and Oglalas looked at each other. Talk about what?

"The railroad is coming," Forsythe continued. "You have all heard about the fire wagons. But some of the Sioux do not want the fire wagons on their land. They fight the railway workers, the surveyors, the men who lay the iron road. Now this is bad. Reasonable men should not fight each other. So the President wants Sioux from each of the tribes—men like White Bull and Two Moons and Blue Horse and the rest of the chiefs—to come to Washington on the cars and talk with him. In that way maybe there can be understanding, and peace."

At first there was hostility toward the proposition. In their measured way each leader got up and spoke his feelings. White Bull said, "Let the President come out here and talk to us!"

Two Moons said, "If we go back there, how do we know they will not grab us and tie us up to make us do what they want?" Blue Horse, after whispered consultation with his nephew, rose to suggest that if he were serious Forsythe himself should come to a Sioux camp as a hostage to guarantee their safety while in Washington.

There was more discussion, but Forsythe finally concluded the meeting, saying, "After you have finished your trading, go back to your camps and think this thing over. There is no hurry. Talk about it, decide on who is to represent you. In August, in The Moon When Plums Get Red, I want your representatives to come back to Fort Jackson. There will be more presents, and wagons to take you to the railhead. You will all get on the cars and go back to talk to the Great White Father. There you will get a lot more presents. They will show you big boats that go on the water and carry hundreds of people, high buildings made of iron, guns that shoot a dozen miles, lights that burn forever on pipes that come out of the walls. You will see all these things, there will be a lot of fine presents. All we ask in return is that you talk with the Commissioner of Indian Affairs and discuss the iron road with him."

When the Oglalas got back to their camp, there was more heated discussion. The Bad Faces favored sending someone to the meeting, but the Midnight Strong Hearts were opposed. Most of the younger men thought it a trick, but some of the elders believed it might be a good idea. The Oglalas had already heard about the daily fighting to the east. Wandering bands of hunters from other tribes passed the word; an old trapper named Ike Coogan, husband to a Brulé woman, told Blue Horse he had with his own eyes seen the shiny rails not a hundred miles from Fort Jackson. Then some of the Slota, half-breed traders the Sioux called Grease People because of the black, sticky stuff they put on the squeaking wheels of their carts, said they had actually seen a fire wagon. It had spit fire and smoke, the Slota said, and made a lot of noise. But many of the Slota were known liars, and no one knew whether to believe them or not. So perhaps, the old men thought, it would not hurt to have some people go and see what the Hat People had in mind. At the very least, the emissaries would bring back presents, maybe even bring worthwhile information to guide them in future confrontations.

Blue Horse asked his nephew's opinion.

"I think," Fox Dancer said, "that it would be good to send some of our people."

Blue Horse puffed at his pipe, enjoying his new supply of Lone Jack.

"What does the three-legged god say?"

"Sometimes," Fox Dancer explained, "it is very hard to talk to. It is just like a woman—it gets mad, and goes for a long time without saying anything. But this time I think it is telling us to go back there. The little blue arrow points in that direction. If that is where the truth is, then that is where we ought to go."

Lightning Man was furious. He sprang up, tearing aside his breech cloth to show his genitals in the supreme gesture of defiance and contempt. "I am a man!" he shouted. "I can do anything! But I do not want to go back there and listen to those Hat People! They are evil! They will give us presents and whisper lies into our ears and put a spell on us! They will try to keep us all inside a fence and put shovels and hoes into our hands to make us farmers!" He raised a clenched fist. "I do not care what Fox Dancer says! I tell you it is wrong to go back there and talk! We will all be sorry someday!"

There was long silence. No one said anything. But after a while the Oglalas made up their minds. They would send a delegation; Blue Horse would lead it. Fox Dancer would go, too. But because Lightning Man and his small following felt so strongly about the matter, it was decided Lightning Man should go also. In that way both sides would be represented.

In The Moon When Plums Get Red they left Fort Jackson in a train of wagons for the railhead. From Elk River's old band of Oglalas there were Blue Horse, Fox Dancer with his three-legged god, and Lightning Man. There were other Oglala chiefs, scalp-shirt men, and important elders from neighboring bands—people like Ugly Face, Cut Finger, and Black Moccasin. In addition, other Sioux groups sent representatives; from the Brulés,

Miniconjous, Sans-Arcs, Hunkpapas, and others, came Porcupine Bull, Bear Louse, Gray Tangle Hair, Broken Dish, and High-Backed Wolf. They were a crosssection of the "hard-case" Sioux whose land the advancing railroad might soon be expected to encounter.

Other important chiefs refused to come in spite of the entreaties of the Commissioner of Indian Affairs and the promises of rich presents. Some distrusted the whole affair, others thought it beneath their dignity to palaver with the white men in Washington. Many sent lesser men and waited for them to return with a report. A lot of powerful figures remained behind, particularly in the Powder River country, men like White Bull, Crazy Horse, and the young but respected warrior, crafty in council and brave in battle, *Tatanka Yotanka*—Sitting Bull.

For the thirty or so that came, it was a time to be remembered. The Indian Commission men who escorted them provided an endless supply of cigars, iced beer, and candies. It was a time for drinking, eating, renewing old acquaintances. For days they traveled on the wagons with a spit-and-polish escort of a dozen cavalrymen, along with a gaggle of newspaper reporters. One of the newsmen later wrote that ". . . it seemed like a gypsy caravan, the Sioux wrapped in red blankets (though the weather was hot), ribboned lances poking into the air, the strange sound of their language as they gossiped and chatted, a long plume of cigar smoke drifting behind as the wagons squeaked and rumbled."

But when they came to the railhead and the cars the holiday mood vanished. The Sioux prowled suspiciously about the steam-chuffing engine, touching hot cylinders and getting their fingers burned. They blinked in sunlight reflected from polished brasswork, gingerly climbed aboard, and examined the steam-pressure gauges and the Johnson bar.

They drew back uneasily, eyes narrowed, when the fireman threw open the firebox door to show them what seemed the flames of hell.

"So this," Blue Horse muttered to Fox Dancer, "is the fire wagon!"

Some of the Sioux refused to go any farther. The whole thing was obviously the work of an evil god. The suspicious ones went around muttering, keeping a wary eye on the locomotive. When the fireman inadvertently opened a valve and blew a hissing blast of steam into a group of them, several ran away, and could not be coaxed back by the Indian Commission men. *Bad*, they signed, holding their fists before them and moving their hands suddenly outward, snapping their fingers. *Bad Evil*. A thing to be cast out, and away!

The bulk, however, coaxed by the Indian Commission representatives, decided to go. Clambering doubtfully on the cars, they settled down for the long ride, wrapping blankets about them and trying to seem unimpressed. Now there were twenty-two, over a dozen having been lost already.

It was dark, about ten o'clock on a moonlit August night, when the conductor swung his lantern and high-balled the engineer. After the long day, and all the food and beer and cigars, the Sioux were sleepy and tired. Suddenly the engine took up the slack in the couplings. There was a great rattling and jerking of the cars, and many of the Sioux ran back and forth in the aisle, frightened. Fox Dancer sat stiffly, pressing his back against the green velour cushion, hands gripping the arms of the seat, not moving. He would not, he decided, move from that seat if *Iktomi* himself came running down the aisle to make faces at him and caper about. Beside him his uncle, Blue Horse, sat as if carved in wood, though his eyes rolled whitely from time to time.

Faster and faster the cars went. As the slack disappeared from the couplings the jerking and iron clashing stopped. There was only a slight forward-to-back motion, in time with the chuffing of the locomotive, not unlike the feel of a galloping horse.

Lightning Man, sitting behind them, said something through clenched teeth.

"Eh?" Blue Horse asked. "What is it?"

Lightning Man's face was pale. "I have ridden a lot of wild horses," he muttered, "but this is the worst! I wish there was some way I could hit it with my whip to make it behave."

Faster and faster the countryside whipped by. In the light of the moon Fox Dancer could see telegraph poles, plowed fields, small white houses with yellow lights. Not red-flickering healthy lights, as a campfire gave, but a sickly yellow-green glow. After a while they needed fresh air; it grew hot and stifling in the cars, especially with the heat from the kerosene lamps swinging to and fro over their heads. But when they opened the windows the smoke and dust were too much, and they closed them again. On they chuffed through the night—passing villages with names like Big Spring, Cayote, Ketchum, Wood River, Silver Creek. Sometimes Fox Dancer could read the names in the light from the locomotive as it curved and twisted ahead; at some stations the station-board was illuminated. Even at that late hour there were curious people standing on the platform to watch the train pass.

Finally, a little relieved, his uncle took out his pipe and loaded it from a fresh sack one of the Indian Commission men had given him.

"You were right," Blue Horse admitted, settling down and pulling his blanket around him. He puffed a shaky circle, and watched it drift upward toward the swinging brass lamp. "I don't know how it works, but this thing does go without horses. And it goes fast."

↔

In Washington it was raining and the city was grateful for the temporary break in the heat. In all the seven wards—from Rock Creek to the poorhouse, from the Arsenal to the Northern Liberties—the Capital had sweltered for weeks. President Johnson abandoned the White House to cruise the Potomac on the *River Queen*. The waters of the river were like pea soup, with a few listless snakes swimming in it, and a new outbreak of malaria was reported from the banks of the old City Canal. No longer used as a waterway between the Potomac and the Eastern Branch, the canal now served as a receptacle for sewage and offal.

The capital was still draped in black in memory of the lately martyred President, and streets thronged with discharged soldiers and officers, unemployed and looking for a job—any job. Kossuth hats, the cartridge box that was the insignia of the XV Corps, red piping of artillery and yellow of cavalry, the acorn of XIV Corps—all these proud symbols now filled public offices and institutions as their owners looked for work; the Patent Office, the Navy Yard, the First Street Prison, the Insane Asylum, City Hall.

Lew Duffy made up his mind that somehow, someway, he would get back into the Army. Mustered out and restless, he had spent all his accumulated captain's pay in what some called reckless living, though he thought it only his due. After all, Duffy had been for a while a brevet colonel, and that gave him a taste for luxury. For a few memorable weeks he lived at Cruchet's Hotel at Sixth and D streets. Cruchet, a French caterer, was the best cook in town, and Lew had put back some of the weight lost in the hospital after Spottsylvania Court House and the confused slaughter at The Bloody Angle. But Cruchet became impatient, and finally angry when Lew's funds ran out. Cruchet threw his baggage onto the street.

"You goddamned frog!" Lew shouted, stuffing socks and underclothing back into the valise. The strap securing it had come apart. "That's a fine way to treat a soldier, a brave man that's shed his blood to save you from the Rebs!"

But Washington was full of brave lads these days; heroes were two dollars a barrel, and a plug of tobacco thrown in.

Duffy strolled over to the avenue to see what he could turn up. A job, he hoped; something to hold him till he could get back in the Army. After that mixup at the Bloody Angle, he was not sure they would take him in again, but the Army was life. He meant to get back in if he had to enlist as a common soldier. In the meantime maybe he would find an old friend from the Iron Brigade who could loan him a few dollars for new boots and a shirt.

After County Monahan and Fort Jackson and places with names like Cold Harbor and Petersburg and Bailey's Creek, Pennsylvania Avenue was another world. Organ-grinders cranked out melodies, fashionable ladies lolled in barouches with black coachmen and footmen. Newsboys bawled the morning papers, urchins swarmed antlike at street crossings, begging to polish gentlemen's boots. Salesmen cried the merits of patent soaps, proprietors of lung-testing machines and telescopes plucked at the sleeves of passersby; at Pennyslvania and Ninth a fruit stand displayed pyramids of pineapples, oranges, and tomatoes. There were the smells of wet, steamy planks from the boardwalks, people, woodsmoke, horse droppings from the new street railway, fresh clay from an excavation into which Duffy nearly stumbled.

Congress was not in session but the avenue swarmed with politicians, Army officers, military attachés from various countries, lobbyists. With cool interest, peeling the orange he had pilfered from a vender's stand, Duffy stared at a French artillery officer in *kepi* and sash, epaulets large and gold-crumbed. A popinjay, really, but the French were good soldiers, though the more dusty and shabby a soldier looked the more likely he was to be dangerous, like the Rebs at the end of the war.

At the President's Park Duffy paused, uncertain which way to turn. As he stood there, deliberating, he glanced to the west, at the half-completed structure of the new monument. A fancy came to please him; in a way, his military career might also be considered only half completed. And in that same westerly direction, beyond the new monument, might lie the balance of his career. The West, now; that was the only likely place anymore to restore and refurbish a military career. Out there on the Great Plains—west.

# CHAPTER NINE

When they arrived in Washington the Great Spirit was weeping. Misty rain fell on the capital. Moisture no sooner touched the streets than it rose again in a dank and miasmic vapor. The air was stifling; not the hard, clear air of the prairies, but a stuff without substance, cheating the lungs, offending the nose.

"They have done something to the wind back here," Speak English growled. He was a Brulé—a short, phlegmatic man whose name was actually Dirty Shirt. But so many of the reporters on the train had approached him asking, "Speak English?" that he finally assumed it was their version of his Sioux name, and adopted it with a certain pride.

Once arrived in Washington, the Sioux were whisked to the Department of the Interior. The Secretary, a bluff and hearty man, welcomed them. White Whiskers, as the Sioux soon came to refer to him, then wheeled abruptly around in his chair, asking, through an interpreter, "Well, what do my red brothers think about the treaty, eh? Are you ready to sign?"

They were startled at such a breach of etiquette. Blue Horse looked straight ahead and said nothing. Ugly Face, squatting on the carpet, wrapped in the best blanket, looked out the window. A fly crawled across Broken Dish's bladelike nose, but he did not stir. Fox Dancer felt embarrassed.

White Whiskers was a busy man who never had a moment to spare. Looking surprised, not managing to conceal his impatience, he repeated his question.

"What do you say, now?" He paused for a moment, looking around. "Well, have you considered the matter?"

The Sioux were tired, hungry, and somewhat confused. In addition, this man was very impolite. Finally Broken Dish, the oldest, got to his feet. Through the interpreter he said, "We are glad to see you. We are glad to be here. We have come a long way in the Great White Father's wagon that rolls and bounces. We are very tired. We will see you in a few days."

White Whiskers was insistent. Ignoring the warning looks of an aide, he said, "I would like to know your decision as soon as possible. After all, the Union Pacific crews are being held up. Every day that passes costs a great deal of money."

Black Moccasin rose. "We are glad to see you," he announced. "We are glad to be here. We have come a long way in the Great White Father's wagon that rolls and bounces. We are very tired. We will see you in a few days."

White Whiskers combed his beard with his fingers in an annoyed gesture. Again he insisted on speedy negotiations. "We are all reasonable men here, you and we," he pointed. "I am sure we can settle this matter quickly. What are some of your feelings, eh?"

Speak English rose, adjusting the folds of his blanket.

"We are glad to see you," he repeated. "We are glad to be here. We have come a long way in the Great White Father's wagon that rolls and bounces. We are very tired. We will see you in a few days."

The Secretary finally threw up his hands and laughed till tears ran down his cheeks and into his cottony beard. He could take a joke as well as the next man, even if that next man was red. He was, he later admitted to reporters, learning patience the hard way.

"All right," he chuckled, shaking hands with the Sioux. "In a few days, eh? Whenever you are ready, gentlemen."

↔

The Government put them up at the Tremont House. They all had individual chambers, and met for meals and discussions in a large room set aside for them. The Indian Commission was generous, and the Indians soon learned that whatever they asked for quickly appeared. Liquors, imported delicacies, cigars—all they had to do was make a mark on a slip of paper. Reporters crowded around, asking their opinions; the hotel management could not do enough for them; the Indian Commission men were courteous and obliging. But Ugly Face and Blue Horse and High-Backed Wolf kept them mindful of what they had come to Washington for.

"First," said High-Backed Wolf, "we must choose one of us to be our chief speaker. We need someone with good words and a hard head. We need someone to argue with the Hat People and make them understand what we think."

After a great deal of argument, they voted on several candidates. Someone—a Sans-Arc chief named Kills Often who sat in a corner and otherwise said little—even cast a vote for Fox Dancer, saying perhaps the three-legged god they had heard so much about might be influential in the treaty discussions. But no one emerged clearly as a favorite until the fifth time, when sentiment swung toward Blue Horse. Finally it was decided; Blue Horse, the respected Oglala, would be their spokesman.

"I thank you all," Fox Dancer's uncle said. "And may The Great One Above watch over us. May he counsel us so that no man here regrets what we do."

Afterward, in celebration, they ordered up a banquet. The management cheerfully set a table in the Grand Ballroom, with gleaming silver and fresh-starched napery. Although the Sioux were not accustomed to such niceties, they did well, furtively watching each other and then adopting whatever seemed to be consensus. Waiters served fresh oysters on a bed of cracked ice, then a clam soup, finally a lobster bisque drenched in butter sauce. A smoking silver platter held a joint of beef swimming in its own juice. There was a nicely browned rack of lamb, and pork chops dipped in egg and crumbs and crisp-fried. At every course a stand was wheeled up with wines in silver ice buckets, and bottles of ale, brandy, and bourbon were passed around. After a profusion of ices, cakes, pies, puddings, and sugared buns the scurrying waiters, threading their way through the squatting, blanket-wrapped Sioux, offered cuts of imported cheese and baskets of fruit, along with iced French champagne. Cigars fol-

lowed, expensive Cuban cigars, and each man took a handful
for later.

Groaning, Speak English patted his bulging stomach. "Buffalo
hump is good," he wheezed, "but there are a lot of things back
here that taste better."

Blue Horse pulled a champagne cork with his teeth and spat
it out, watching as the contents of the bottle foamed up and ran
down his hand. "I wish we could learn to make this stuff," he
said. "I hear they brew it from grapes." He turned to his
nephew. "Do you think we could make it from wild grapes?"

In spite of his stomach trouble Blue Horse had sampled everything, particularly a lobster stew rich with cream and butter
and laced with hot peppers.

"I don't know," Fox Dancer murmured. "Perhaps."

He himself had not eaten a great deal. After a while he got
up and went to the window, staring out at the sheets of misty
rain. It was getting dark; carriages rushed to and fro in the street,
lamps reflected a yellow glow from pavement puddles, a bedraggled cat foraged in an overturned trashcan. He did not like this
place, did not like Washington at all, but had a sense of forebod-
ing not shared by the rest of the Sioux. They ate long after ap-
petites were satisfied, stuffing food into mouths, opening bottle
after bottle of brandy and cognac, giggling and saying crazy
things and playing jokes on one another. After a while some got
sick and vomited. Others toppled over and went to sleep on the
floor. Even Blue Horse seemed to be in a stupor and finally
dozed where he sat, an empty bottle in his lap and a half-eaten
pastry in one hand.

For a long time Fox Dancer watched. Then he stepped carefully among them, making his way toward his room. As he left
the Grand Ballroom he was aware of his cousin standing in
the doorway, watching also. Lightning Man must have known
what he was thinking.

"Don't look like that!" Lightning Man growled. "It is their
right! The white man owes them a lot."

Fox Dancer could only shrug and walk away down the freshly
painted corridor with its thick carpeting and flowers in vases.

He was anxious to consult his three-legged god and see what it thought of Washington.

↔

The first meeting with the Government officials came only after a week of palavering among themselves as to a unified position. White Whiskers pressed them, but Blue Horse was adamant. "First," he insisted, "we Sioux must meet, know each other, talk about a lot of things. When it is time, we will come."

Finally it was time. Uncomfortable in chairs, the Sioux sat in their finery around a big table in the auditorium of the Interior Department. Blue Horse was especially impressive, clothing and manner setting off well the tall, lean body, the strong head and jaw. In spite of the clinging heat he wore his best buffalo robe, and his red leggings were beautifully worked with beads and shells and ribbons. From the single eagle feather in his black hair to the richly embroidered moccasins, he was a man to be reckoned with.

The Indian Commissioner, a friendly, black-bearded man named Wingate, welcomed the Sioux. Blue Horse made a dignified speech in return. He waved away the Indian Commission interpreter and signaled to Fox Dancer to put his words into English.

"I hope," Blue Horse said, "that the Sioux can be friends with the Hat People. That is the way it used to be. In our Winter Calendar there is a Winter When The White Men First Came. That was a long time ago. At that time, when he came in his canoe, the white man was not very big. His legs cramped him because he sat for so long in that little canoe, and he begged us for a piece of land to light his fire on. But when he got warm, and when his belly was filled with the meat we gave him, he got very big. With one step he walked across mountains. His feet were so big they covered the Indian's plains and valleys, pushed down forests, scared away the buffalo. His hands took hold of the eastern seas and the western sea at the same time, and his head rested on the moon."

Wingate and the Indian Commission men listened respectfully. The Army was well represented too, but many of the blue-

clad officers looked bored. One said something behind his hand
while the other smiled.

"Now," Blue Horse went on, "the Great White Father says
he loves his red children. But I am not sure I believe him. Sometimes I think he is really saying 'Get a little farther away or I
will step on you.'" Blue Horse paused and looked around. "Is
that the way a father talks to his children?"

President Johnson had sent a representative, too, but the spec-
tacled man did not seem to be watching; instead, he was busy
writing in a little book.

"Anyway," Blue Horse concluded, "we ought to be friends. A
father should be friend to his children, and the children should
look on their father as a friend, too. So I hope that we will all
be friends, and that we can work out some way we can live together." He threw out his arm in a sweeping gesture. "For
friends," he said, "there is always room."

It was only the first of interminable meetings. Nearly every
day the Sioux got into carriages and rolled grandly down the
avenue to the Department of the Interior, where they sat for
hours in the musty interior while the Indian Commissioner and
Blue Horse debated. Earlier feelings of goodwill and amity began
to dissipate, and the Sioux almost broke out into rebellion when
an Army major, impatient at the haggling, said that force would
have to be used if the Sioux did not listen to reason. It took
three days and a lot of talking to entice the angry Sioux back to
the conference table. A higher authority relieved the major from
further participation in the talks.

Blue Horse became querulous and annoyed. His stomach was
hurting him, too. "Why do they not show us the paper they
wrote the treaty on?" he asked his nephew. "Why are they holding it back? They tell us all the time what they are going to give
us, but what do they want?"

"I do not know," Fox Dancer admitted.

One night there was panic in the Tremont House. Speak English turned on a gas jet and then went to look for a match. By
the time he found one the room was filled with gas, and the
unfortunate Brulé blew out three windows, set the room on fire,

and was taken to the hospital with severe burns. The incident only increased the edginess of the Sioux delegation.

The talks dragged on. Days passed, then a week, then two weeks. Many of the Sioux delegation lost interest in the talks, if not in the free food, liquor, and tobacco. Even when the Department spokesmen finally produced a draft of the treaty, barely half could be mustered to attend the important meeting. Some were on a trip to the Mint, where they received shiny new silver dollars. The Friends of the Indian had taken several to the Deaf and Dumb Asylum, where the Sioux were delighted to find they could converse easily with the inmates by means of their sign language. Lightning Man and some of his adherents had gone in carriages to the Navy Yard, where officials were going to demonstrate the fifteen-inch Rodman gun, firing it down the Potomac to show how far it could shoot. Fox Dancer, acting as deputy for his uncle, finally managed to round up enough of them and together they went to the Department of the Interior to hear the reading of the proposed treaty.

Mr. Wingate beamed at them over his spectacles, and his staff smiled. The Government, he said, was pleased to make such a magnificent offer to the red men. They were to be given a reservation on the Powder River, which would be theirs in perpetuity. No white man, no railroad, was ever to breach that sacred land. The Sioux could continue their wild and free life in a land teeming with game, fish, birds, all the good things of earth and sky. For those who were interested, there would be Government schools to teach reading and writing and arithmetic. A man could raise corn and beans, there would be free seeds, hoes, even plows and teams of horses. Others might want to learn the trades of carpenter, mechanic, or blacksmith. The Great White Father would send people to teach them. In addition, after the treaty was signed, there would be magnificent presents; Texas steers for meat, shelled corn and beans, rice, dried apples, tobacco, saleratus and salt and pepper for seven generations to come. The Government would build real white men's houses on the reservation for all who wanted them, complete with shiny furniture, dishes, and pictures. The list went on and on;

bolts of calico, axes, mirrors, beads, black powder, lead of bullets, knives.

The Sioux returned to the Tremont House, carrying printed copies of the proposed treaty, which most of them could not read. They depended on Fox Dancer to interpret the writings and the maps, and felt dazed and confused. Everything had happened so fast; Mr. Wingate had spoken so kindly and reasonably; the irritating Army major had been removed; in many ways the proposed treaty seemed acceptable. After all, they did not often stray far from the limits proposed on the map, and there were all those presents. But—how was a man to know?

"I do not trust them," Lightning Man insisted. "It is a long list of presents, yes. But we have never been fenced in, like cows. What happens when we have eaten all the corn, smoked the tobacco? What happens when the horses die, and the white men's houses they give us get old and fall down? What happens when the women have used up all the bright cloth, and the mirrors are broken and the beads scattered and lost? What happens then?"

No one knew quite what to think. But when Blue Horse tried to get Black Moccasin and Broken Dish and a few of the wiser heads together to discuss the treaty, most had left in a carriage for a banquet the Friends of the Indian was giving for the red men. At first the Sioux were impressed by everything they saw in the Capital; the iron ships at the Navy Yard, the new street-railway with its jingling bells, the tall buildings and the crowded streets. But now they were more sophisticated. It took something exotic to hold their interest, and the banquet offered to provide it. There would be, a Friend reported, a fountain that spurted champagne. They knew champagne and liked it. So Blue Horse, tired and ill, went to bed.

In fact, Fox Dancer himself had recently to take on more and more the brunt of stating the Sioux position, often adding to or subtracting from his uncle's words. Sometimes he simply put forward ideas of his own which seemed good. Sometimes Army or Indian Commission interpreters, jealous, perhaps, frowned at his translations and whispered to each other. But the young man was Blue Horse's nephew, and Blue Horse obviously trusted him without reserve; moreover, Blue Horse was the key to the treaty.

If it did nothing else it improved his skill at English. Now Fox Dancer could read printed material fairly well, and the desk clerk at the Tremont House always bought the *Evening Star* and the *Daily Chronicle* for him and sent them up. From them he first learned of the considerable local sympathy for the Sioux, and the support of certain powerful organizations. It helped their bargaining position. Still, there was strong opposition to any peaceful solution of the "Sioux problem." The Sunday morning *Chronicle* printed a poem by an aroused Methodist lady which ended by referring to the visiting Sioux in terms of:

> "A *stony adversary, an inhuman wretch*
> *Incapable of pity, void and empty*
> *From every drachma of mercy.*"

That night he had a strange and disturbing dream. He was once again a boy, watching the foxes dance. But when the foxes discovered him this time, a beautiful fox with a brush that shone healthy and sleek took his arm and danced with him. When they had finished, this fox pulled him close and whispered into his ear.

Fox Dancer didn't understand, and asked, "What? What?"

Then the fox faded away. He was sitting up in the strange and unaccustomed bed, staring into the night, listening to sounds of late revelry from the rooms down the hall where the rest of the Sioux stayed: Porcupine Bull, Bear Louse, Broken Dish. He heard clinking of bottles, drunken shouts, giggling and laughing. Children! he thought angrily. The Hat People are making fools of us! His uncle Blue Horse stirred on the floor, where he insisted on sleeping, and coughed. Blue Horse no longer seemed able to keep order among the delegation. He was very tired, and sometimes spit up bright patches of blood.

Disturbed and thoughtful, Fox Dancer went to the window and looked out. Nothing; the walkways shone white and serene in the moonlight, a late breeze ruffled the dark leaves of trees, the gas-lamps still burned. But having dreamed of foxes, and waked uneasy, he began to think of Lew Duffy. Always he carried the *picksher* with him, rolled in a cylinder in his medicine bag. Lighting a candle, he took out the "picksher" and studied it. Somehow, he wished he could talk to Lew Duffy. Here, among all these strange and threatening white faces, with such a difficult decision to reach, it would be comforting to talk to the red-hair man. Oh, Duffy was vain and foolish, and a braggart! But Duffy was also a brave man, and a kind of bond of foxes was between them. Fox Dancer believed Duffy would tell him the truth, even if it was only the truth according to Duffy. If nothing else, Duffy was honest.

↔

Colonel John Logan, USA, also wanted to see someone. He had heard that his old friend was in town; knowing his quarry well, Logan started searching in saloons, bars, card rooms of hotels, brothels. He also spread the word among his acquaintances who had served in the Iron Brigade. It was important that he find Lew Duffy, and fast. Even since he had mentioned Duffy to General Cardwell, Fancy Dan had given him no rest. Cardwell's idea might work, it might not—John Logan was against it on principle, if for no other reason—but a general's whim was a staff officer's order. So Logan kept looking, and started others searching also.

He suspected Duffy had run by now through any Army pay he had left, and expected to find him now in dives even worse than Marble Alley. It was true. One rainy August morning Logan found him being thrown out of a seedy and flea-infested bagnio called The Haystack; Lew Duffy, boots split, hair and beard long uncut, uniform coat torn and soiled. Duffy brushed the dust from the seat of his pants, muttering an Irish curse.

"Lew! Lew Duffy!"

Duffy turned, startled as if the Metropolitan Police were after him. Recognizing an old friend, he smiled sheepishly, uncertain and embarrassed.

John Logan took him by the arm. "By God, Lew, you're a hard

man to find!" He stood back, looking at Duffy. "Don't look to me like times are good with you!"

Duffy had his pride. "Oh, I'm temporarily down on my luck," he admitted. "But things are sure to pick up. In fact, I was just on my way to see a big factory owner about a job in his foreign-trade department."

Logan knew Duffy of old. "I don't believe a damned word of it," he snorted. "Look, are you interested in getting back in the Army?"

Duffy dropped his pretense and clutched him by the arm. "Listen!" he said hoarsely. "Listen, John! If you could—if you could—"

Logan didn't say anything, only looked at him. Actually, the colonel was thinking of the depths to which an impulsive man could fall. But Duffy misinterpreted the silence.

"I know I pulled an awful boner," he said sadly. "That business at the Bloody Angle—at the time I thought it was a great idea, John. Believe me, a man doesn't often have a chance to be a hero and maybe save the whole damned Union at one and the same time. But—"

Logan shook his head. "I wasn't thinking about that—at least not right now. No, the job I have in my mind wouldn't be affected by that." Reaching into his wallet, he took out the administrative funds General Cardwell had authorized, and handed Duffy five ten-dollar notes. "Take these," he ordered, "and clean yourself up. Have your blouse sponged and pressed, get a haircut and a trim, buy some new boots. Come in to the War Department at Seventeenth and F at eight in the morning sharp. Ask for me—I'll be waiting."

Duffy's eyes misted. "John," he said reverently, "I haven't seen that much money in a year!"

"Never mind that!" Logan said sharply. "I don't want you to disappoint me now—remember that! Eight in the morning!" He turned to go, but added, "By the way, where are you staying? In case I need to find you again."

Duffy held up one of the ten-dollar bills. There was a light in his eye. "Willard's," he said. "On Fourteenth Street. By God, tonight I'm going to have an oyster supper, and champagne!"

At ten minutes before eight, he was outside Colonel Logan's door, a different man, alert and confident. New boots were polished to a mirror finish, fresh blue piping adorned his breeches, hair and beard were neatly trimmed. John Logan looked him up and down, approved, and took him in to see General Cardwell.

"Thank you, John," Cardwell said, and motioned to Logan to leave them alone. Then he said, "Sit down, Captain."

It had been a long time since anyone had called Lew Duffy *Captain.*

"John Logan has told me all about you," Cardwell went on.

Duffy did not speak, reminding himself that a junior officer used his voice only to answer questions, especially in the presence of general officers. And Fancy Dan Cardwell, as Logan had called him, was the most general of general officers. He wore a uniform that took Duffy'e eye; a nonregulation and apparently custom-made rig with sweeping collar points and a red kerchief knotted around his neck. The shoulder boards were heavy with ornament, and the burnished silver stars large and adorned with what looked like precious stones. Cardwell himself was a dark and intense-looking man with an Assyrian profile, a wreath of curly hair surrounding a pale, aristocratic face.

The general went on, delicate fingers playing with an inkwell that had two stars engraved into the base. "A rash type, are you, Duffy?"

Lew was startled. "If you mean about what happened at Spottsylvania Court House—"

Cardwell shook his head. "I know all about that. War Department files are very complete. At the Bloody Angle you thought you saw a chance to be a hero, and started a foolish charge against a Rebel battery after being specifically instructed to hold your ground and wait for reinforcements."

Duffy didn't say anything; that was the truth of it.

"Should have had a court-martial!" the general snapped. "Damn foolish thing! If all hadn't been so confused, and you wounded and shipped off to a hospital, there *would* have been."

He revolved the inkwell delicately, careful not to spill ink. "No, that's all over, water over the dam. But I trust you learned something from that, Duffy. To follow orders. To do what you're damned well told!"

Duffy swallowed. "Yes, sir."

"Logan tells me you lived with the Sioux back in sixty-four."

"Yes, sir."

"Got to know them pretty well, eh?"

"Yes, sir."

"Speak Sioux?"

"Fluently, sir. I—I studied languages at Trinity."

The general laughed. "And ran away from Trinity, too, when you got into a scrape!"

The War Department files were indeed extensive. Duffy licked his lips and muttered, "Yes, sir."

From a table the general picked up a copy of the *Evening Star* from the day before. A smudged headline of large size said SIOUX UNCERTAIN ABOUT SIGNING TREATY. A smaller head said *Government Officials Impatient.* "Been following this?" Cardwell asked.

Duffy peered at it. He had not had the price of a newspaper for a long time. "No, sir," he said. "I—well, there were other things on my mind."

There were, indeed. But SIOUX UNCERTAIN ABOUT SIGNING TREATY? What Sioux? What treaty?

"Well," Cardwell said, "the damned Sioux are in town, haggling with the Indian Commissioner. Wingate wants to buy 'em off with a lot of presents, get 'em the hell out of the way of the Union Pacific. That's what the talks are all about."

"Yes, sir."

"Goddamned bloody savages!" the general barked. "Did you see 'em the other day when the President had them to the White House to give Blue Horse that big silver medal?" Not waiting for an answer, he went on, pacing about the room, hands clasped behind his back. "Enough to make a soldier sick! President's Park full of soft-headed people, all applauding and grinning like baboons! Sioux, mind you!" He shook a finger at Duffy. "Murdering Sioux! Well, there's only one way to handle a Sioux, my lad! You shoot him before he shoots you, and lifts your hair into the bargain!"

He sat down again, leaning back in his chair, dark eyes still angry. "Though I shouldn't take on so," he said. "It's just that the goddamned Army has to sit with its mouth sealed, its hands tied! They won't let us speak or act except at the discretion of the Indian Commissioner! And all *they* do is give the red bastards presents and try to wheedle 'em into signing a treaty! Good God, what does a Sioux know about a treaty!"

Blue Horse, Duffy was thinking. Blue Horse and maybe some of the Oglalas are here to talk about a treaty. He wondered if Fox Dancer was in Washington, too. Beginning to get a feel for the situation, he murmured, "Not much, sir. I mean, I guess an Indian wouldn't be likely to know what signing a treaty meant."

"Right," Cardwell said. "Exactly right." He took out a gold watch from his waistcoat pocket. "Got a meeting with General Sheridan at ten," he said. "Have to hurry. Now listen to me, Duffy. The war's over, isn't it?"

"Yes, sir."

"What's a good soldier to do, now there's no more war?"

"I've been wondering, sir," Duffy said.

"Right, exactly right! A soldier's meant to fight. That's his life, his career, the way he gets tin on his shoulder boards, eh? So you and I, we've got to keep on fighting, or we don't get anyplace. Now where do we fight?"

Duffy took a long shot. "Out on the Platte," he said. "We fight the Sioux."

"Right," the general agreed, slapping the desk. "*That's* why the Army doesn't want any foolishness about a damned treaty! What better service can the Army offer to the country, eh, than to smash the Sioux for once and for all? Make a better land for all of us, free of bloodshed and obstructionism and naked red savagery?" He leaned across the table, staring hard at Lew Duffy. "You were breveted colonel once," he said in a low voice. "How would you like to have those silver eagles back?"

Duffy swallowed hard and sat straight in his chair. "Sir, just tell me what I have to do!"

"At those treaty talks," Cardwell said, "the Army is under strict wraps. We're allowed to send observers, that's all. We tried to start a little trouble between the Indian Commissioner and the Sioux—I sent Major Larkin over to threaten force if the red bastards didn't sign—but the Commissioner managed to butter it over and get the Sioux back to his meetings. Now Intelligence says the Sioux are on the fence about the treaty—some want to sign, some don't. So you"—he stabbed out his finger—"you, Captain Duffy, are going to be our new representative at the meetings. You know Blue Horse and his people, you speak their language, you lived with 'em and know their ways, their weaknesses. I want you to stay with 'em, be useful to 'em, get their confidence. And as a good Army officer, I trust you to use that confidence discreetly to persuade them *away* from the treaty."

"Yes, sir."

"And remember this! If anyone gets suspicious of you—if the Indian Commissioner or any of his people or any goddamned nosy reporter gets wind of what you're doing, I'll disown you! I'll say you were off on a toot of your own, and the Army washes its hands of you! Not only that, but there may be a court-martial convened to look into that action of yours at the Bloody Angle. Understand me?"

"Yes, sir," Lew Duffy said. He did in fact understand, and was frightened but elated.

"You're dismissed!" the general said.

Though he had not expected to meet his old Oglala acquaintances until the next morning, Duffy saw them somewhat earlier. Lying between clean sheets at Willard's, stomach full of oysters and still pleasantly giddy from champagne, he woke at the knock on his door. It was still dark, perhaps five, and the clerk held a candle for him to read the note:

SOME KIND OF SIOUX TROUBLE AT TREMONT HOUSE.
GET DOWN THERE INSTANTER AND SEE WHAT GOOD
YOU CAN DO FOR US

Across the bottom, in bold, slashing script, was the signature *Daniel Cardwell, Major General, USA.*

# CHAPTER TEN

Blue Horse was dying, there could be no doubt about that. At three o'clock of an August morning, heat still radiated from the walls of the hotel; the day had been hot and stifling, the sun a brassy disk, air fetid and damp. Now Blue Horse lay wrapped in his blanket on the floor, gasping for breath and bleeding from the mouth. Lightning Man, crouched in the light of a candle, from time to time wiped Blue Horse's lips. The cloth was already sodden with its burden of blood.

"Can you speak, Father?" Lightning Man asked. "What do you want? Can we do something?"

Blue Horse's stained lips could not form the words he wanted. He only looked fondly at his son, then closed his eyes. His lungs rattled with the effort of breathing.

Fox Dancer squatted beside his cousin. They were all there in the room—Speak English, Broken Dish, Ugly Face, Black Moccasin—except for a few who were too drunk to understand that their leader was dying. "Maybe," Fox Dancer suggested, "we ought to say to the clerk downstairs we need a doctor—a white-man's doctor."

Blue Horse managed a great effort. "No!" he cried. "No! I do not want a white-man's doctor!"

Lightning Man wept. It was the first time Fox Dancer remembered seeing tears in his cousin's eyes. "He is right," Lightning Man muttered. "What do Hat People doctors know about the Sioux? My father will go in his own way, when he wants to."

A few minutes later Blue Horse died. There was a gush of blood from his mouth, a strangled cry. That was the end of Blue Horse, respected successor to Elk River, a father and wise counselor to his people and to all the Sioux.

"He is gone," Lightning Man mourned. "He is gone up into the Milky Way, to the Camp of the Dead. We will not see him anymore. We will not see anyone like him anymore."

They needed white sage and red-willow bark to burn for the death ceremony, but none of these essentials was in the Hat People's city. So the Oglalas had to content themselves with chants, and praying. After a while they decided to bury Blue Horse.

"But where?" Speak English asked. He had been drinking whisky and his speech was slurred, gestures erratic and uncertain. "Where are good trees—old and beautiful trees to do honor to him?"

Fox Dancer took the nearly empty bottle of liquor from Speak English. He protested, but Fox Dancer threw it out the window, saying, "That stuff is poison, brother. Poison like the rattlesnake. We have to stop drinking all that bad stuff, eating all that bad white-man's food. Maybe that is what killed our father here."

For a while they haggled about details. They were practical enough to know that in the Washington heat something would have to be done quickly. Fox Dancer kept quiet while his elders were talking, then said, "I know a good place. It is called the President's Park. Do you remember the time the Great Chief of the Hat People gave our father that big silver medal? Well, in that place, right by the lodge where the chief lives, there are a lot of fine trees. I do not think their chief will care if we bury Blue Horse in his trees."

It sounded like a good idea. Someone pulled down the heavy oaken poles that supported the curtains, with the idea of making a litter to carry Blue Horse. But Lightning Man objected. "He carried me on his back when I was a child," he said. "Now I will carry him."

They took hatchets and knives and went down the dark stairs, a long column of painted Sioux with Lightning Man at their head, carrying Blue Horse on his back. At the desk a clerk was reading a newspaper in the sickly light of a gas globe. He looked up, his mouth dropped open.

"Here, here!" he cried. "What's all this, now? What's going on?"

Fox Dancer explained politely that Blue Horse had died. They were on their way to bury him.

The clerk was upset. "You can't do that!" he protested. "There's got to be an inquiry—the District Coroner will have to examine the body and determine cause of death—why, there are all sorts of papers to be filled out!"

"I don't know about that," Fox Dancer said, still polite. "But we are taking him to be buried. That is all I have to say."

The clerk stood in the doorway, holding up his hands. "Now just a minute, gentlemen! Maybe we can talk this over. It's bad for the hotel, having someone die here. If you'll wait till I can wake the manager and—"

They pushed by him and walked out onto the avenue. It was still dark, though in the east there was the gray of false dawn. Gas lamps hissed their yellow glow, cobbled streets shone damply, from the trees came a drowsy chirping.

"This way," Fox Dancer ordered.

An iron fence surrounded the President's Park, and the gate was locked. High-Backed Wolf broke the lock with a swift blow of his hatchet. They went in, carrying the corpse, moccasins making dark streaks in the wet grass. Finally they found a likely tree—a tall and sturdy oak near the south portico of the White House.

When they started to chop down branches to make a burial platform, the noise aroused a watchman, who came running from the lower floor of the White House.

"Good Lord, it's those Indians! They're chopping down the tree!" he cried.

The Oglalas looked briefly at the watchman, then went on with their chopping and trimming of branches. Baffled, the watchman pointed to where Blue Horse lay, wrapped in his best red blanket, Presidential silver medal gleaming on his chest in the half-light.

"Who's that?"

"He is our father," Fox Dancer explained, cutting a stout

branch to size with his knife and weaving it into the platform they were fashioning. "He is dead now. We are going to bury him in this fine tree. Now go away and don't ask questions!"

"You can't do that!" the watchman protested. "Besides, you're trespassing!"

Some Metropolitan Police, alerted by the clamor, came into the park, approaching the Sioux from the other direction. "Hey, Harry!" one of them called. "What the hell is going on here?"

Harry welcomed the reinforcements. "These people are cutting down a Government tree!" he complained. When Black Moccasin made a threatening gesture with his hatchet the guard shrank back. "You saw him!" he cried. "He threatened me!"

The situation was becoming dangerous. Fox Dancer tried to explain what they were doing, but the watchman was insistent. The Metropolitan Police drew their weapons. "You're trespassing, and maybe endangering the President! Anyway, you can't bury a dead man here—it's against the law. Now get out, quick!"

Ugly Face rushed toward the police, hatchet upraised. But a blue-coated figure ran between them and knocked up the weapons. "Now wait a minute!" the officer cried. "Wait a damned minute, will you?" He turned to Fox Dancer, speaking in Sioux. "Brother, I am glad to see you again." He made the sign for *heart*, then the circular gesture for *sun*. *Sunlight in the heart. I am glad to see you.* The officer was Lew Duffy.

"It has been a long time," Fox Dancer agreed. He went quietly back to his cutting and trimming while the others fitted branches and boughs into a kind of bed.

"Listen here," Duffy told the police. "I wouldn't bother them, if I was you. They're apt to trim your ears with a hatchet."

"But it's against the rules!" the watchman protested. The Metropolitian Police agreed. "There are all sorts of District regulations about cadavers, and don't none of 'em say you can bury anyone in a tree."

Duffy was persuasive. "These are important people." He pointed to the silver medal on Blue Horse's chest. "The President himself gave that to the old man. Just move over there,

along the fence, and keep your mouths shut. I'll take full responsibility for everything."

"Who the hell are you?" someone asked.

Trim and natty in his new uniform, Lew Duffy drew himself
up. "Captain Lewis Duffy, special representative of the War
Department to the Indian Commission and the treaty talks
that are now going on," he announced. "Now get the hell away
and let me straighten this out!"

The eastern sky brightened, showing streamers of red and
yellow and gray. Birds began to chirp drowsily in the trees.
Duffy made a ritual sign toward the dead body, then squatted
on his heels, watching the Sioux put the platform in place
among the lower branches of the oak. They lifted Blue Horse
reverently to lie among the green leaves, the chittering birds,
tucking the red blanket under and around him as a mother does
her infant. They stuck a sapling into the ground beside the tree,
and tied the old man's sash and rattle to it. Then they all sat
down in a circle and had a smoke. Fox Dancer gestured to Duffy.
The Irishman strolled over and sat with them, silent, accepting
the pipe each time it came around. From the fence the watchman and the police looked on, impatient and worried.

After a while old Broken Dish muttered, "It is hard to bury
a man in a place like this. Too many people. They all give us
trouble."

Lightning Man agreed. "But it is all over now. *Wakan Tanka*
has taken our father up in the sky where his stomach will not
hurt him anymore."

They smoked for a long time. Lights winked on in the White
House. One of the police called something to Duffy, but the
Irishman did not respond; the red-hair man only smoked, stolid
and patient as the rest.

High-Backed Wolf said, "Blue Horse always looked out for
the enemy and did something brave. He studied everything and
tried to understand it. He kept an even temper and never was
stingy with food. He was useful and renowned among The People, and that is all I have to say." *Finished,* he signed.

Fox Dancer agreed. "We have no leader," he said, puffing at

the ornamented pipe. "Our father has gone to see *Wakan Tanka*. We are a long way from home, among strange faces, strange lodges. We do not know what will happen."

Duffy blew smoke to the four corners of the earth in honor of the dead man. His Sioux was far from perfect, but understandable, especially with his fluent gestures. "Over there, in that big lodge"—the Irishman pointed toward the White House—"The Great White Father is getting up to drink his coffee. He will be very sorry to hear Blue Horse is dead."

No one spoke.

"He will be sorry, too," Duffy went on, "that he was not able to do great honors to Blue Horse."

Again they said nothing, only smoked in silence. The light quickened, a shaft of sun probed through the chimneys of the White House and lay on the upper branches of the oak tree.

"You have already buried Blue Horse," Duffy continued. "That is all right. But I do not see any reason why the Great White Father should not bury him too. That would make everybody happy."

Lightning Man's face was impassive. Sometimes his broken fingers still pained him; he hated Lew Duffy. But there was a question in his eyes.

"The Great White Father," Duffy explained, "would put Blue Horse in a box of polished wood, with a plate on it telling of his great deeds. There would be handles on the box to carry it, silver handles, bright and shiny. He would put Blue Horse in a coach wagon with glass windows and little doors and soft cushions, drawn by beautiful black horses. A lot of important Hat People would walk after the coach. They would all go to a place called a *cemetery*, where they would put the box in the ground with other brave men in boxes so they could all sleep together."

Ugly Face took out his scratching stick and worked a while at his scalp. Finally he demanded, "They would do all this?"

Duffy made the *truth* sign, moving his thumb outward from the chest to show that the words came directly from his heart. "I have spoken only truth."

Lightning Man went to stand at the base of the oak tree,

looking upward. His lips moved but no one could hear him. Finally he returned and sat down in the circle.

"There are no Sioux in that burial place?"

Duffy shook his head. "But brave men are brave men. There is no color to the skin of a brave man. Blue Horse will be happy in the cemetery."

While they considered this, the rising sun cast the buildings along the avenue into bold relief against a cloudless sky. It would be another hot day. Finally they all got up. Fox Dancer knocked dottle from the pipe, saying, "All right. Friend, you fix everything for us. Agreed?"

Duffy nodded, right hand held level and flat, palm down, near the heart; then sweeping it away and out. *Agreed.*

The next day the old man was buried with great ceremony. The Government laid him to rest against the red brick wall of the Congressional Cemetery, overlooking the Anacostia River. Senators, Congressmen, Friends of the Indian, high-ranking Government officials attended in great numbers. White Whiskers himself delivered an elegy to the Oglala statesman. The Sioux were greatly pleased with the ceremony. Fox Dancer felt pleased, too, and grateful to Lew Duffy.

↔

The Washington *Evening Star* put the matter succinctly in a headline; THE SIOUX PROBLEM——WHEN WILL IT BE SETTLED? Following was a long and peevish article about lack of progress in signing a treaty. The editorial writer was sympathetic about the death of Mr. Blue Horse, the Oglala chief. But he pointed out that it was only another of the interminable delays which marked the whole affair. "The Nation," the *Star* concluded, "cannot be expected to endure much more of the charade. It is up to all parties concerned—the Army, the Indian Commission, the railroads, and the Sioux themselves—to realize that speedy action must now ensue. Time is running out."

The Sioux agreed. They were tired of Washington; after almost a month they heartily disliked the heat, the crowds, the malarial air, the bustle and clatter of the avenue that kept them from sleeping at nights. They were split on the matter of the treaty; a faction under old Broken Dish was ready to sign in exchange for the generous presents. The other faction, nominally under Black Moccasin but drawing most of their arguments from Lightning Man, did not want anything to do with the treaty. But no action could be taken without a leader.

Gloomy and dispirited, they squatted in a circle, passing around the pipe and trying to figure out what to do. "I do not like all these people looking at us!" Speak English said in disgust, glowering at the spectators who ringed the room behind a restraining rope. "How can a man think with all that noise?"

The Tremont House management was charging twenty-five cents to the public to see the Sioux, but they could not really object since Ugly Face astutely demanded that half the receipts be shared with the Sioux.

"We have to think anyway," Black Moccasin insisted. "Who would make a good leader? We have got to finish this business and get away from this bad place."

The Sans-Arc chief, Kills Often, spoke up. Usually he sat in a corner and took little part in the discussions, but now he said, "I want Fox Dancer to speak for us."

It was a strange idea. After all, Fox Dancer was the youngest. Even Lightning Man was older.

"I don't know about," Black Moccasin objected.

Broken Dish snorted. "I have a grandson older than Fox Dancer!"

But Speak English pointed out something important. "Yes, Fox Dancer is young in years." Then he tapped his head. "But up here he is very old and wise."

"That is right," Kills Often agreed. "And anyway he has been speaking for us all along."

Lightning Man was annoyed. "What do you mean by that?"

Kills Often, angry at Lightning Man's abrupt manner, refused to say anything more, putting thumb between first and second fingers and pushing it at Lightning Man in a gesture of contempt. But Speak English took up the argument. "It is easy to see what he means," he explained. "Everyone knows Blue Horse

was old and sick, and at times he could not think clear. Everyone knows a lot of the words Blue Horse said were really the
words of Fox Dancer. That young man is really the one who has
been telling the Hat People the truth about the Sioux, how we
only fought and took scalps when the Hat People came into our
lands and killed the buffalo and dug up the ground and tried to
plant corn and beans where our fathers are buried."

Broken Dish nodded. "Yes, that is so. It is something to think
about."

Lightning Man was still angry. But it was an idea whose time
had come. Most now agreed that it had been Fox Dancer all
along who had steered the talks, who had spoken for the Sioux,
who had skillfully avoided the traps the Government laid for
them. And it was Fox Dancer who owned the white man's
three-legged god. Not everyone acknowledged its efficacy, but
none wanted to challenge it. In the end they all, even Lightning
Man, agreed that Fox Dancer would be their leader until the
talks were concluded.

In relief, Broken Dish and some of the others planned a feast
for that night. The Tremont House laid in a lavish supply of
champagne, bourbon, rum, and brandy; John Welcher's restaurant, on the Avenue, catered a dinner of oysters on the shell,
chicken cutlets, sweetbreads and game, ices, jellies, charlottes,
candied preserves, cake, pie, fruit, candy, tea, coffee, along with
four kinds of French wine. But Fox Dancer remained in his
room. Their choice of him as leader surprised him. It was a
frightening responsibility. He prayed for a long time to the Great
One Above for wisdom. Then he turned to the Hat People god
for guidance. But the god was not helpful. The glass clouded,
and the needle swung erratically this way and that. Angry, he
almost struck it with his fist, then reconsidered. After all, the
fact that he could not at this moment get a response did not
necessarily mean anything. Had he not wished Duffy to come?
And Duffy had come. Perhaps the god merely worked in its
own way. For a god, that was reasonable.

Relieved, he went down to the common room, where the feast
was taking place. From far away he could hear clamor and con-

fusion. When he entered, no one paid any attention. Thick with cigar smoke and whisky fumes, the room trembled with noise: shouts, curses, drunken laughing, clinking of glassware. The Sioux staggered about in a welter of broken and empty bottles, remains of left-over meals. Piled along a wall were wooden boxes filled with ribbons, laces, and fancy edgings. In a corner was heaped a selection of cloaks, opera hoods, military toys, and cigar cases they had bought at Boswell's Fancy Store for souvenirs, and the Indian Commission had paid for. Old Broken Dish swayed up to him, pulling the cork from a fresh bottle of sour-mash bourbon.

"The Hat People have *some* good things!" the old man giggled, draining a quarter of the bottle in one breathless gulp. His eagle feather was awry; somewhere he had lost a moccasin.

High-Backed Wolf had a pot of imported fish eggs under his arm, eating it with a big spoon. His face was smeared with the little black eggs. "This is very good," he said, offering some to Fox Dancer.

The young man pushed the spoon away but Lightning Man staggered near, having trouble getting the cork from a bottle of French champagne. He leered at Fox Dancer, eyes trying to focus, then complained, "I cannot get the cork out of this bottle, cousin. Will you help me?" He hiccuped, grinning foolishly.

"I will help you," Fox Dancer said, "I will help all of you." Angrily he grabbed the bottle and threw it against the wall. It broke with a loud report, and foam spattered the grapevines and pink roses of the wallpaper.

For a moment the hubbub ceased. Necks craned, bottles were lowered, in surprise High-Backed Wolf dropped his pot of caviar. It showered his moccasins with clinging black eggs.

"What did you do that for, cousin?" Lightning Man demanded.

"Because," Fox Dancer said coldly, "you are a fool!" He swept his arm wide in a gesture to take all of them in. "You are all fools! The Hat People have made you so!"

Lightning Man, sobered, drew his tasseled knife. He looked at the shattered champagne bottle, still spinning on the carpet amid shards of broken glass.

"I did not give you leave to take that bottle from me!" he shouted.

Broken Dish spread out his hands pleadingly, gray hair disheveled and face smeared with berry pastries. "Brothers, brothers!" he quavered. "Listen to me! This is no time to fight! We are having a good time! Let us—let us—" As he spoke his old legs betrayed him. Slowly, slowly, he went down to the floor. As he collapsed his hand grabbed the spattered linen of the tablecloth. Bottles, tureens, silver, crystal, chafing dishes—all crashed to the floor.

"I do not fight with anyone here," Fox Dancer explained. He went to a table, selecting a fresh, unopened bottle with each hand. "I fight only this enemy!" he cried, hurling the bottles at the wall. They burst noisily; beads of whisky and crumbs of glass spangled the air. "I am tired of seeing my brothers drink this poison and act like children," Fox Dancer shouted. He smashed a bottle of raspberry cordial against the wall, and purplish syrupy stains stitched down the flowered paper. "I am tired of seeing my brothers fat and drunk, my father, Blue Horse, sick and dying with rich foods, all of us forgetting our own people back there." He gestured westward, picking up an armful of bottles of Penniman's Best Dutch Lager. "And I am tired of myself, and ashamed I did not speak sooner!"

A knock sounded at the door but no one moved to open it.

"I am a young man and respect the elders, but I have to do something to stop all this and remind us we are important people! We are people who came a long way to speak for the Sioux! Have we forgotten that?"

"What's going on in there?" a worried voice inquired beyond the door. "This is the manager!"

Fox Dancer locked the door. Then he folded his arms and looked at the Sioux. That was all he did: looked.

Broken Dish was the first to move. Shakily he pulled himself upright, leaning on the table. With a sleeve he wiped at his stained mouth. "Maybe," he muttered, "maybe you are right."

He hiccuped, putting a hand to his stomach. "I do not feel very good anyway."

High-Backed Wolf wiped fish eggs from his buckskin shirt, looking sheepish. Speak English blinked like an owl, looking down at the bottle of rye whisky in his hand as if he did not know how it had gotten there. Ugly Face had his hands in a large cake decorated with pink and white flowers, and he slowly withdrew them, wiping hands on his leggings.

Slowly the tide turned. "That is the truth!" Kills Often cried. He ran to a sideboard, gathering bottles of French brandy in his arms. "Did I not tell you?" he demanded. "This young man always speaks wisely!" The first bottle he threw was off target, and only fell to the floor. But the second one hit a gold-edged mirror, and bottle and mirror both shattered with a satisfying crash.

"Metropolitan Police!" someone yelled, pounding with a fist. "I order this door to be opened!"

Gleefully the rest of the Sioux took up the new game. They scattered, looking for bottles, carafes, platters of game and meat, jars of preserves and fruits—anything to throw.

"Fox Dancer is right!" Speak English howled. He lifted the lid from a silver tureen. "This excrement makes me sick! It is not fit for any man to eat!" He flung the contents against the wall. What looked like lobster and clams and oysters in a rich sauce clung for a moment, then oozed slowly down.

"It is time," Black Moccasin shouted, "that we acted like Sioux, not like Hat People!"

Even Lightning Man agreed. He forgot his injured pride and put away his knife. Taking an armful of cordial bottles from the food-spattered table, he threw them out an open window, shouting, "*Onhey!*" the ancient Sioux battle cry. "I have overcome the enemy! Look at me, brothers, how I destroy!"

That was when the door splintered, falling inward with a crash. Blue uniforms of Metropolitan Police swarmed into the room, followed by the frightened manager of the Tremont House. Astonished hotel guests and servants peered in through the wreckage of the doorjamb.

"Good God!" the manager cried. "What happened? What *happened?*"

Fox Dancer spoke for them all.

"We are Sioux again," he said. "And we will not forget it."

# CHAPTER ELEVEN

It was late September—*The Month When The Wild Rice Is Ripe*. But there was no wild rice here, only sticky heat varied by thunderstorms that cleansed the air but left the next day more uncomfortable.

Lew Duffy attended the treaty talks as the Army's sole observer, but said little, only giving information to the Indian Commission when asked. Fox Dancer spoke to the Irishman occasionally in a corridor; they talked about old times on the frontier. The red-hair man had mellowed, even joked about being traded for "three plugs of cable twist tobacco and a packet of needles," as he put it.

It must have been apparent to Duffy how divided the Sioux remained on the treaty, but he did not mention it. Fox Dancer wished that Duffy would show how he felt, but the Irishman preserved strict neutrality. Fox Dancer thought better of him for it. It meant Lew Duffy was not trying to prejudice him one way or the other.

In their brief talks Fox Dancer said nothing of Shell or her baby. Someday soon he might ask Duffy his honest opinion about the treaty. He did not want the Irishman then to be influenced by any consideration of his one-time woman and a child in an Oglala camp. But the precaution was unnecessary. Duffy never mentioned Shell, not once, and of course he did not know about Sun Hair.

Still, something had to be done. The Sioux could not stay in Washington forever. The year was running out; already they should be in the winter camps, storing meat and dried vegetables and nuts and berries against the coming cold. Yet there was no consensus.

"I say touch the pen!" old Broken Dish insisted. "There are more Hat People than there are blades of grass! I have fought all my life. Now that I am old and have some brains in my head, I see there is a time to make peace, too. Look at the big guns the Hat People showed us! They shoot a long way! And all we have to do is touch the pen! Then they will give us horses and beeves and calico and flour and things."

Black Moccasin shook his head. "I do not want to be told where to live! I do not want to ride after a buffalo and see a white man's fence in my way. I like presents, yes. But I do not want to trade our land for bright red cloth and a few hatchets!"

Angry, Lightning Man sprang to his feet. "We cannot give away land that belongs to Rock and Thunder and the Sioux gods! It is *their* land! We are only keeping it for them! The gods will be angry if we trade it to the Hat People!"

Broken Dish took out his scratching stick, poking it into his gray locks. Finally he asked, "What will we do then—fight? I do not mind fighting the Crows. They fight our way, we all know the rules. But the Hat People and their fire wagons and big guns—"

"I have seen their big guns!" Lightning Man shouted. "The biggest one cannot shoot all the way back to the Powder River! I am not afraid of big guns!"

It was an impasse, and they turned to Fox Dancer.

"What do you think, my son?" Broken Dish asked. "We do not want to do the wrong thing. Whatever we agree on, here in this room, can mean living or dying for the people. What do you say?"

Fox Dancer lighted the ceremonial pipe, passing it around the circle. Outside the window carriages rolled along the avenue, hooves clip-clopped, a newsboy with brazen lungs pressed the *Evening Star* on passersby. No breath of air came through the curtains, and he felt beads of sweat on his forehead and chest and arms.

"I do not know," he admitted. "I had a lot of dreams when I could not sleep at night. But no dream is clear, tells me what to do."

"Ask the three-legged god," Lightning Man jeered.

It was bad manners but they were all irritable and upset.

"That god does not want to talk," Fox Dancer explained. "I told you before—sometimes it talks a lot, sometimes it gets mad and will not say a thing. Just like a woman who is mad at her husband. But I have other medicine."

They were curious. "What? What medicine?"

Fox Dancer shook his head. "I cannot say now. But tomorrow, after I have done some things, we will talk more. I will tell you then what we should do." *Finished,* he signed, and would not say more.

At supper he did not join the rest, but sat silent and alone in his room, staring at the Hat People god. He felt like shaking it, kicking it, maybe throwing it out the window. But what to do? How advise his people? There could be only a single answer: sign the treaty, or not sign the treaty. Broken Dish was right. Whatever they did would affect the lives of Sioux for generations to come. The responsibility laid heavily on Fox Dancer's shoulders. He could, he knew, persuade the delegation either way: to sign the treaty or reject it.

Twilight came; still he sat cross-legged in the center of the room. He thought of that day, long ago, when he had stood outside Elk River's *tipi*, looking at the Oglala land—his land. The pine trees had darkly pierced the blue, clouds sailed like boats, the ponies pulled grass with their big teeth while trout jumped in the dammed-up pond. He remembered the feeling that swelled up in him that day, the feeling his heart was too big for his chest. He and The People and the land and the animals and the gods were one; the ponies, the sky, the ripples in the pond, the V-flights of geese honking far overhead, Thunder, Rock, all the rest. From that feeling he had gotten satisfaction, a sense that all was harmony, that the Oglalas were safe in the hand of the Great One Above. Vainly he tried to recapture that feeling, the comforting knowledge that he and his actions and his life formed part of a great whole, that he and the Sioux moved along a course the gods favored.

But in this smelly place, this crowded and noisy capital, Fox

Dancer could not recapture that feeling. It was gone, completely gone; his heart was empty. Tortured, he put his head in his hands, staring at the familiar pattern of roses and vines on the carpeting. He put down his hand and touched it. Nothing there; nothing but hard, dusty threads. No, a man must touch the earth. But where was the earth? Everything was covered with buildings and paving blocks and sidewalks and rugs. Where was the earth?

Finally, he knew what he had to do. In response to his request, the obliging desk clerk sent a messenger to find Captain Lewis Duffy and bring him to the Tremont House.

↔

The fox-haired man was diffident and pleasant. "Nice place you got here," he murmured, settling in the chair Fox Dancer indicated. Fox Dancer himself folded his legs and squatted on the floor. It was late, well after nine in the evening. The hanging lamp—what the Tremont House management called "the expensive new Rochester harp-type lamp"—cast a yellow glow and made jagged shadows on the papered walls.

"I want to talk to you," Fox Dancer explained.

"All right."

"You know we have a big question to decide. It is a matter of to sign the treaty or not. Sometimes the gods do not speak and we do not know what to do. Sometimes it is hard to decide, because a lot of important things might happen—bad things, if we do not decide right."

Duffy grinned. "I've been listening to you in the treaty talks, friend, and you've come a long way, that's a fact! But you never did understand adverbs. Don't say, 'if we do not decide *right*.' Say, 'if we do not decide *correctly*.'"

"I do not know about the way I talk," Fox Dancer said. "But I know about the way I think. And I think I want to know what the red-hair man says about the treaty."

Duffy frowned, twirling his blue cap on the end of a finger. "What do *I* think?"

Fox Dancer nodded. "What you think."

Duffy shook his head. "I'm only an observer at the meetings. I'm not supposed to have opinions."

"This," Fox Dancer said, "is only between us."

Duffy seemed uneasy. "Listen, if it ever came out I talked to you in private here at the Tremont House, I'd be in trouble. You know damned well old Wingate is death on the Army! He thinks we've interfered enough already." Again he shook his head. "It would be my head served up on a silver platter if I said a damned word to influence you people!"

Fox Dancer respected Duffy's position. It must be difficult for someone who liked to talk as much as Lew Duffy to sit day after day in the treaty hall, unable to speak. Especially it must be difficult with Duffy himself, one of the few there who knew the Sioux, had lived with them, understood the Sioux way of thinking and acting.

"Are you afraid?" Fox Dancer taunted. "Is it your skin you want to keep whole?"

Duffy must have had a sharp answer but he bit it off and looked at his twirling cap. "I'm a soldier," he growled, "I've got my orders, you know that!"

"I know," Fox Dancer agreed. "And you must be a good soldier! You have two silver bars now, not just a gold bar. But I want to tell you something."

Duffy looked at him, suspicious.

"When we caught you that night," Fox Dancer went on, "a lot of the people wanted to kill you right away. Lightning Man hated you. You did something to his fingers one time, and they still hurt him and make it hard to hold a gun. But you ought to remember one man said, 'no, do not kill the red-hair man.' A certain person said, 'take the fox to our camp.' That person saved your life, and when it came The Moon When Corn Is Planted, we took you back to Fort Jackson."

"That's true," Duffy muttered.

"So one man saved your life. And it is a little thing, for a man's life, to ask him how he feels about a treaty. So: is it a good thing for the Sioux to touch the pen? Or is it a bad thing, a thing we would be sorry for later?"

Duffy was upset. He rose to prowl about the room, hands locked behind his back. The harp lamp shone redly on his ringlets, disturbed from running his fingers through them in agitation.

"Sweet Jesus, that's a hell of a position to put me in!" he blurted.

Fox Dancer said nothing, only watched him.

"You know," the Irishman protested, "I could get in all sorts of trouble!"

Fox Dancer shrugged. "A man gets in trouble sometimes. It is part of being a man. But if you are afraid of trouble—"

"It isn't that!" Duffy snapped. He sat down again, crushing the cap in his hands. "You know goddamned well it isn't that! It's just that—" He broke off, staring down at the crushed cap. "I've worked hard for these captain's bars, and I don't want to risk them! But anyway—" He broke off again, then slapped his knee hard with the cap. "All right, then! I'll tell you what I think! But don't ever let anyone know I said this!"

Fox Dancer nodded. "I understand."

"Shake hands on it?"

They shook hands.

"All right," Duffy said. "Don't sign the damned treaty!"

"Don't sign?"

"No." Duffy wiped sweat from his forehead. "I've always respected you people. Oh, I tried to kill as many of you as I could, once, and I put in some uncomfortable times in your winter camp. And I was damned mad when you bartered me like I was a slave! But I respected you, the way you live. You're wild, free people. If they try to shut you up in a reservation, don't let 'em do it! You'll die—you'll not be able to breathe! Forever free, that's what you ought to be!" The Gael, the poet, was coming out in Duffy's words. "Live like men, damn it! Then, if you have to, die like men!"

He paused, catching his breath. Fox Dancer said, "I know that way to live. It is the way we have always lived. But what good is the world if there are no Oglalas? What good is a world where a man's family—his wife and his children—were killed by the guns of the Hat People? What good is a sun, and the wind, the stars, and buffalo hump roasting over a fire, and smoking a pipe with your friends, when there is no one to see these things with you, to—to—"

Duffy helped him. "To enjoy them with."

"Yes, to enjoy. What good is that?"

"All right, then," Duffy agreed. "But what good are these things if a man has to live like a horse in a corral, tell me that! To live behind a fence, to plow up the ground and plant corn and beans like the Rees? To be half a man—a gelding, a fat steer? What good is that?"

Fox Dancer was silent.

"Anyway," Duffy went on, "I don't think you need to worry. If you don't sign the treaty, the world isn't going to come to an end. Turn it down, see? Go back to your own country. My guess is they'll leave you alone—just route the Union Pacific around you. Anyway, even if they do send troops after you, there are one hell of a lot of Sioux. Fight them, they'll respect you more!" He made a sharp gesture. "Hell, look at the Rebs! They fought us for four years, and killed hundreds of thousands of poor boys in blue. But Grant gave the Rebs their horses back at Appomattox, and old Lincoln said we wasn't mad at 'em no more! Now the Rebs are getting fat and sassy again! No, sir—stand up for your rights, be men! Someday you'll be glad you did!"

It was late; the clock on the wall ticked ponderously. For a long time they sat together, neither saying anything. Finally Fox Dancer rose, pulling his blanket tightly about him. He felt cold; there was a hollow feeling in his stomach. But he took Lew Duffy's hand, saying, "*Hie, hie!* I thank you for what you have told me, friend."

Duffy was still agitated. He jammed the cap on his red curls and paused at the door. In the lamplight his face was white. "I—I—" He broke off, rubbing a boot toe in the thick pile of the carpet. "Goddamnit, I didn't want to talk to you, remember that, will you?" His voice rose to a shout. "I didn't want to tell you anything!"

Fox Dancer touched him on the shoulder. The gesture was tentative, almost shy. "Don't worry," he said. "I will not tell anybody." He made the ritual gesture for *truth*, thumb pointing stiffly outward from clenched fist, then moving the hand rapidly forward. *Straight out, directly from the heart.* "You have told the truth. A man does not need to be ashamed of telling the truth."

The Irishman gave him a long, anguished look. Then he rushed down the hall, hurrying boots silent on the thick nap of the carpeting, and turned the corner, not looking back. But Fox Dancer, watching him go, saw something else. In an alcove off the hall, a small bay window filled with ferns in pots, a man was talking to old Broken Dish. As Duffy hurried by, the two of them withdrew into the shelter of the greenery.

The man looked like one of the Indian Commission interpreters. And it appeared he had been handing something to Broken Dish; a small, paper-wrapped parcel.

↔

The next morning Fox Dancer called the Sioux delegation together. He told them what the Hat People's three-legged god had said. "It was hard," he explained, "and I had to promise three medicine lodges before the god would talk to me. He had been angry with us and would not speak because he did not like the way we ate rich food and drank liquor and acted the fool. The god does not like the way his own Hat People act either, trying to make us touch the pen for a few gifts and presents— maybe money too." He looked at Broken Dish but the old man did not meet his eyes, puffing instead on his pipe and staring out the window. "The god," Fox Dancer went on, "thinks it is evil to try to buy us so. Finally he spoke to me. And this is what he said."

They were silent, expectant; even Lightning Man was attentive.

"The three-legged god," Fox Dancer said slowly, "tells the Sioux not to touch the pen, ever! The god says we are free people, forever free." Fox Dancer used Duffy's own words. "We should go back home, get ready for winter. We should pray to Rock and Thunder and the Great Ones, sharpen our knives and hatchets and make lead bullets for our guns. Then, if the Hat People are angry and come against us in the spring, if they bring fire wagons any farther into our land, then we should fight. That is what the three-legged god says!"

There was a hubbub of excitement, disagreement, shouts of approval, some of anger. Broken Dish threw away his pipe in a shower of sparks. Burning crumbs of tobacco fell onto the carpet and glowed, but nobody paid any attention.

"I do not believe that god!" Broken Dish shouted. "Brothers, don't pay any attention to Fox Dancer! That Hat People god has taken away his brains! He talks like a fool! Listen to me! If we touch the pen, we can have all kinds of good things! Beer and plenty of tobacco; horses, wagons, good beef, a lot of calico for the women! We can have—"

Black Moccasin shouted him down. "You foolish old man!" he roared. "Just because you are soft in the head, do you think the rest of us are fools? Maybe someone as old as you, with no teeth, needs Hat People beef! But brave men eat buffalo hump, and do not need wagons to ride in!"

Gray Tangle Hair was put out by Black Moccasin's lack of courtesy. "You should not act that way toward Broken Dish," he grumbled. "He is an old man, honored and very wise. You should never—"

Porcupine Bull broke in, "This is no time to worry about being polite! We are talking of The People, what is to happen to them, will The People live or die? Do we fight like men, or do we sit inside a fence and let the white man put a collar around our necks, the way they do with horses that pull plows?"

Gray Tangle Hair shrugged, looking sad. It appeared there would be few dried apples or raisins in Sioux camps anymore. Gray Tangle Hair liked dried apples and raisins as much as Broken Dish liked white man's beer. Even Black Moccasin, having second thoughts, asked, "If we fight them, what about all their guns? What about—"

Fox Dancer made a quick motion with his hand.

"Is a brave man like Black Moccasin afraid of guns? The more guns, the more chance to count coup!"

Kills Often agreed. He made the sign for *exterminate*—flat of one hand rubbed briskly several times across the open palm of the other, making a dry, rustling sound. "Wipe them out!" he shouted. "That is what I have said all the time!"

There was much argument. Broken Dish made a long speech, favoring the treaty, and was angry when people kept breaking in with comments. Lightning Man made a fighting talk, declaring that he would never become a farmer, as the Hat People wanted, planting beans and corn behind a fence; he would die first. But after a while a general agreement began to appear. The Sioux liked the good things the Hat People could give them, but they loved freedom more. Finally, late in the afternoon, they voted to reject the treaty.

Whether the decision proved to be good or bad, they now felt a sense of relief. There was no further need for tedious meetings with the Indian Commission, sitting hour after hour in the Great Council Hall of the Hat People, listening to haggling better suited to women arguing over a scrap of cloth or a handful of carved-bone buttons. No, it was better this way. Now they could go home, back to the good country.

Lightning Man came hesitantly to his cousin, taking Fox Dancer's hand in his own twisted fingers.

"I am glad," he said simply. "Maybe I did not trust you, cousin, because sometimes you think too much, and do not listen to your heart. But this time your heart has spoken. *Hie, hie.*"

Afterward, Fox Dancer asked the Indian Commission for a big meeting. He made an eloquent speech refusing the treaty, a speech people remembered for a long time.

"We are free people," he said, "and must be forever free! If we go to a reservation, like you want us to, we will all die. The Sioux are things made by the Great One Above, just like the grass and trees, the animals, the clouds, and the sky. Can the Hat People talk to the grass and tell it to go someplace else and grow? Can the Hat People tell the clouds to stay in one part of the sky? Can the Hat People tell the water in the streams to stop running, to turn around and go someplace else? The Sioux are no different from all things the Great One Above made. We have to do what the Great One planned for us, that is all I can say. He made us free; we are going to be free—free forever."

In spite of their disappointment, the Friends of the Indian, the Commissioner, many Government officials, and newspaper reporters were impressed by the eloquence, the clarity, the beauty of Fox Dancer's speech. In later years, someone guessed, it would go down in history with the orations of other red men who had come to Washington to plead their case—the Seneca Red Jacket, rugged old Chief Pushmataha of the Choctaws, even the great Black Hawk, the Sac, who years before reminded some of President Madison in demeanor, style, logic. FOREVER FREE, a headline in the *National Intelligencer* said. *Moving Speech by Sioux Chief Before Indian Commission.* But most of the newspaper comment was outraged. *Sioux Refuse Treaty. Bloodshed on the Frontier. New Killings. Government Action Long Overdue.*

Fox Dancer himself said little, but carried a burden no one suspected. The three-legged god had not advised him as he claimed. The god had not really told him anything; Fox Dancer had lied to get his way. Lew Duffy was really the one who had advised him. And during the speech the Irishman sat silent and morose in the back of the hall, chin propped on hand, a lonely spectator.

Still, Fox Dancer told himself, it was not all that bad and dishonest. In his mind Duffy and he were inextricably linked. He and Duffy were fox brothers—he had known that from the first time he'd seen the red-haired Duffy, panting and disheveled in the firelight of the Oglala hunters' camp. After all, maybe the god had not spoken directly to Fox Dancer. On the other hand, the god had brought the Irishman when Fox Dancer needed him. It was evident that there was a mystic bond between Fox Dancer and the Irishman. Maybe, just maybe, that was truth enough.

↔

They left Washington in a chill rain. The station was filled with smoke, smelling of cinders, hot oil and steam, people. In contrast to their coming to the Capital, the Sioux were being hurried out of town with little ceremony and less luxury. There were no more free cigars and beer, no liquor, no attentive Indian Commission escorts. Only one man attended them, and he did not care a great deal what happened to them.

Standing on the platform, wet and miserable, they pressed together in a group, aware of hostility that surrounded them. Passersby eyed them with distrust; a black-shawled woman shook her fist at them and called out a curse; one man said his nephew was in the Sixth Cavalry and had been killed by Indians on the plains.

Porcupine Bull sighed damply, saying, "They want to get rid of us any way they can! The soldiers want to kill us their way. The Indian Commission wants to put a fence around us and kill us that way. I guess we cannot please the Hat People except to lie down and die."

The trip seemed endless. By the time they got to Chicago they were hungry, and the Indian Commission man gave them only enough money to buy a few loaves of bread and some sausage, saying it was all he had. When Fox Dancer went to buy a newspaper in the station, a crowd of sullen people followed him. One jeered, "Look at the monkey—thinks he can read!"

After a while the Sioux turned sullen and perplexed. The Indian Commission man left the train in alarm, and refused to come back. Fox Dancer was thinking of raiding a station restaurant in Clinton, Iowa, when Broken Dish came to sit beside him under the swaying oil lamp.

"Here," the old man said. He handed Fox Dancer a soiled wad of bills. "Take this! Buy us something to eat."

Fox Dancer looked up in surprise. There was over a hundred dollars in the packet.

"Where did you get this?" he demanded.

The old man looked embarrassed. Then he grinned and scratched his head. "*Iktomi* tempted me once," he explained. "He came to me in the hotel back there." He pointed eastward. "*Iktomi* said he would give me a lot of money if I would talk to my brothers, make them understand how good a treaty would be."

"I see," Fox Dancer murmured.

When they reached Fort Jackson after several jolting days on the wagons that met them at the railhead, they found that Colonel One-Arm Forsythe had been retired from the Army. The adjutant called Henry was running the post pending the appointment of a new commanding officer. As the Oglalas rode away on the ponies kept for them during the trip at the Eighth Infantry stables, Fox Dancer paused at the top of a rise and looked back. It was late afternoon; golden shafts of light painted the stockade walls, the red, white, and blue flag hung limply from a tall pole. It was quiet, very quiet; the post and all its outbuildings seemed like a scene painted on a drum.

He would never see Fort Jackson again. He would never come there again to trade or parley. From that time on, Fox Dancer knew, there would be war between the Hat People and the Sioux.

# CHAPTER TWELVE

Late in September Fox Dancer and his people trotted down through the pass from the north and entered the Oglala winter camp. The camp dogs heard them and came running and barking, followed by bands of excited children. Later, as the delegation rode into the sunny valley, the older people ringed them, shouting, "*Hau, cola!*" Fox Dancer looked in vain for Shell; he wanted to see her gentle face but she was not in the throng.

Rejoicing was short-lived. Fox Dancer told them of the death of Blue Horse, in the great city to the east, and the Oglalas who had remained in camp were plunged in grief. Women gashed their arms and legs; Twin Woman cut off her little finger with an ax in sign of mourning; the Midnight Strong Hearts and the Bad Faces held a special ceremony, marching about the camp carrying the dead man's war bonnet, his gun and bows and arrows. They also carried his pipe and tobacco, and other items Blue Horse especially favored. As the procession passed, people sat before their lodges, faces smeared with ashes, singing songs of the soldier bands to which Blue Horse once belonged; the Owns Lance Society, the Strong Hearts, the Bad Faces.

The ceremonies lasted for three days. After that, according to their practice, all of Blue Horse's property was given away. This was the custom only for brave men who had died in battle and not returned, but they all understood that Blue Horse had given his life for them in a kind of battle with the Hat People back in Washington. Finally his *tipi* was torn down and burned and the name of Blue Horse was never mentioned again. He had gone up through the Milky Way to the Camp in the Sky and taken on a stature that made it sacrilegious to mention his name among earthbound men.

There was a council meeting among the warrior societies to decide who should take Blue Horse's place as *wakicunza*. Many candidates were put forth, but only one commanded real support. In The Moon When The Wolves Run Together, Fox Dancer, in spite of his youth, succeeded his uncle as camp chief of the Oglalas.

"I am very happy you have come back," Shell told him.

On a cold night they sat together in Fox Dancer's *tipi*, watching the baby toddle excitedly about the lodge, his tiny body casting shadows on the walls. Sun Hair was walking, though only ten months old. He stumbled, fell, still laughing, and Fox Dancer picked him up and put him on his feet. It was getting cold, and he threw a stick of wood on the fire.

"I am happy to come back," he murmured. He wanted to add "to you" but was embarrassed. Still, he was with Shell and the feeling was good.

"I missed you," she said shyly.

He did not look at her, only at the fire. "And I you."

He thought of Lew Duffy, and Shell's devotion to the Irishman. He did not tell her he had seen Duffy back in the great city. Duffy had not even mentioned Shell, and his absence of feeling would hurt her.

Then she crept beside him, laying sleek braids on his shoulder. "You will not go away again?"

He trembled a little, hoping she did not feel it. The gesture was a sisterly one, a thing a girl would do for a loved and respected brother. But in spite of his best efforts he became angry.

"How do I know?" he shouted, and stalked out of the lodge, leaving Shell and the baby staring in surprise.

Outside, a blanket-wrapped figure squatted, watching a disk of yellow moon that hovered over the trees. In the hills to the north a wolf howled, then another. The night was crisp and cold, and the smell of snow was in the air.

"Do you want something?" Lightning Man asked.

Since Fox Dancer's election as *wakicunza*, Lightning Man

had appointed himself personal aide. Though refusing to enter the lodge where Shell and her baby lived, he sat for long hours outside the *tipi*, waiting for the *wakicunza* to command him. He elected himself hunter for the household, daily bringing haunches of deer, fat rabbits, and delectable bits of liver and kidney and heart. He never spoke to Shell, leaving the meat outside for her to find.

"Is something wrong?" Lightning Man asked again. "Cousin, what is the matter?"

"There is nothing the matter!" Fox Dancer shouted, and stamped into the woods, away from people.

↔

That autumn some others came to join the Oglalas. A few Hunkpapas entered the winter camp, bringing dogs and children and women. Their name meant *End of the Circle People*, from their insistence on camping always at the end of the circle of lodges, at the point of greatest danger. There were a few Brulés, too, and some Miniconjous; even a small band of disaffected Crows, who had heard of Fox Dancer's proposal that they join forces against the Hat People.

"For," old Bent Nose, leader of the Crows, said, "there is going to be a big fight. They have a new chief at Fort Jackson, a chief with a shiny star on his shoulder. I have heard he wants to fight us, wipe us all out!" The old man made the palm gesture, scowling. "That is what he wants to do!"

"This Star Man," Fox Dancer asked. "Do you know his name?"

Bent Nose didn't know. "Anyway," he said, "Star Man will have to wait until the snows go away. I think we should make plans for a big fight when spring comes."

The Oglalas usually laid by what seemed a reasonable amount of food; corn, beans, dried meat, buffalo butchered and put into the ground to freeze. But the memory of the past hard winter was still fresh. So they stored extra food, and when the first snows came they were snug and warm in camp. There was not much to do except eat, sleep, smoke, and play cards with greasy decks Fox Dancer had brought back from Washington.

At times the new *wakicunza* called the warrior societies together, along with the visiting Brulés and Miniconjous and Crows. They talked about how to prepare for the certain spring offensive against them by the Star Man at Fort Jackson. But there was plenty of time for details; the meetings served more to pass time than to effect any real planning.

Though the first snows had come and several inches blanketed the valley, the Slota, the Grease People, came by in their carts to trade. Necessities provided for, the Oglala now bartered furs and hides, extra meat and corn and beans, for Slota goods; cloth, mirrors and beads, even a small keg of rum. Fox Dancer frowned on this latter exchange, insisting on keeping the keg in his own *tipi*, to be used only for ceremonial occasions.

The Slota, after spirited bargaining, had time to sit down and smoke a pipe. They, too, brought news from the post.

"A lot of pony soldiers are there," Jean Richaud said. He was half-French, a fat and jolly man with dozens of black-eyed children peering from his wagon. "Oh, a lot more than there have ever been before. *Mon Dieu*, something big will happen this spring! I think they are planning to drive all the Sioux clear into Canada, to make room for their big railroad that will soon come whistling and tooting and chuffing smoke!"

Sometimes, when she was very lonely, Shell spoke of Duffy. It made Fox Dancer angry but he tried hard to hide his anger, only sat silently when she talked of the Irishman.

"He was so funny," Shell remembered. "He had jokes to tell, and he played a lot with the children. Sometimes I wake in the middle of the night, and feel he is near me." Her eyes filled with tears, and she quickly went to rocking Sun Hair in his crib of buffalo ribs and hide.

"Why are you crying?" Fox Dancer protested. Desperately he wanted to touch her, to run a hand across the sleek braids, but did not dare. Instead, he covered his emotion by speaking crossly. "There is nothing to cry about!"

Shell dried her eyes on the sleeve of her beaded shirt.

"Sometimes," she explained, "I wish he could see the baby."

Before the big snows, old Ike Coogan and his Brulé wife struggled through the northern pass to visit. The main entrance to the winter camp, the one the hunting party had taken when they brought Lew Duffy in as their prize, was now entirely closed. The narrower and more difficult northern pass was still negotiable for a knowledgeable and mountain-wise trapper like Ike Coogan.

"*Hau, cola,*" Fox Dancer smiled, handing the old man a fat and crackling buffalo rib from the fire.

While his Brulé woman sat patiently in the shadows the trapper gnawed on the bone, whiskers dripping with shiny fat and bits of meat. Finally he wiped his mouth with his sleeve. The buckskin was so old and dirty that it shone. Coogan smelled bad, too. The Oglalas bathed often in summer, even in winter washed themselves from a basin of warm water. They kept themselves clean, and Ike Coogan's smell offended them. But he was a good friend to the Oglalas, and Fox Dancer squatted patiently while the trapper sipped at his tea.

"On my way to winter diggins," Coogan finally belched, putting down the tin cup. "Me and my woman."

"Yes."

"Going to be a hard winter. Got a peck of beans or so you could lend me?"

Fox Dancer made the sign for *yes*, raised index finger suddenly bent in simulation of a standing figure bowing, agreeing.

"Corn, too, if you need some," he offered.

"That's moughty generous of you," Coogan wheezed. "In my book you're one of the good ones, sonny." He accepted the pipe, saying, "Member that red-headed mick stayed in camp with you last winter?"

Fox Dancer glanced at Shell. She was wiping the baby's bottom with a handful of grasses; anyway, she did not understand much English.

"Yes."

Coogan puffed a ring of smoke. "Mighty good 'baccy," he said. "You bring it from Washington with you?"

Fox Dancer made an impatient gesture. "You were talking about Duffy, the red-hair man."

Coogan took another reflective puff. "The Irisher is back in the country again."

"Duffy? Where?"

"At the post," Coogan said. "They got a new gin'ral there, you know. Brass butt named Cardwell—some call him Fancy Dan. It ain't usual for a small post like Jackson to have a full gin'ral commanding; probably means big action in the spring."

"But about Duffy?"

Coogan nodded. "One of the cavalrymen there—feller named Schmidt, from E Troop—my God, I never seen so many yellow-legs in my life—anyway, this here Schmidt says Captain Duffy is the real brains of the place. Cardwell is just a big blowhard, 'thout sense enough to come in out of the rain. But Duffy, Schmidt says—Duffy is the one that's planning mischief. Duffy is the one that knows Sioux; Duffy's the one that knows how to hit 'em hard and make it hurt."

Duffy! Lew Duffy! The red-hair man, back in Oglala country again! Fox Dancer felt a cold sensation in his stomach. He hardly heard Coogan as the old man rambled on.

"Duffy's kind of dog-robber for the gin'ral, I guess. Oh, he was always a sly one! I seen that last winter when I dropped by your camp. Never trust a mick, that's what I allus say! Why, in Omaha once, when I was a young man . . ."

Fox Dancer wasn't listening. The decision to refuse the treaty was, of course, his own; he had advised the Sioux delegation, no one else had, and the decision was his responsibility. The red-hair man had spoken only under duress.

"Duffy!" Fox Dancer murmured.

Ike Coogan looked puzzled. "Eh?"

"Duffy," Fox Dancer repeated. "He is really here."

"Shore 'nough."

It was ironic; Duffy advised the Oglalas to fight. Now Duffy was at Fort Jackson to fight them. But the Irishman had only been sent by the War Department, the way a soldier is sent anywhere. What was more reasonable than that he be sent to the frontier, where his knowledge was useful? The Great War the Hat People fought among themselves—that was finished. Now a soldier had to go wherever he was ordered.

"Thanks, sonny." Ike Coogan rose to go, motioning to his woman. "We got to rustle our butts or we'll get froze to death on the trail." After he shook hands with Fox Dancer, the old man wiped his leathery palm over his arms and chest. Ike had lived a long time with the Arapahoes. It was an Arapaho gesture, one of respect; it meant *There is good in you, knowledge, a big heart. I want some of that on me.*

"Hie, hie," Fox Dancer said in farewell. But his voice was absentminded; he hardly noticed when Coogan and the Brulé woman slipped out of the *tipi* and rode away in a downpour of white.

A day later there came the first heavy snow of the season, a blizzard with driving wind behind it, sweeping across the hidden valley so hard that flakes skimmed horizontally like small white birds. Over a foot of snow fell in one night, and when the snow stopped the temperature went down very far. After a few days the wind died and a misty sun appeared, with a colored ring about it. This was a good sign to the Oglalas; the people walked about the village in winter clothes, visiting, chatting, exchanging gossip. Old Bull Head, the crier, trotted around camp on his pony, hands over his ears to protect them from his deep-mouthed shouting. "There will be a Clown Dance tonight by the Heyoka Society. In the morning all women gather wood. Fox Dancer says the Miniconjou and Brulé and Crow friends are to come to his *tipi* at moonrise to make plans for the spring. Shell needs extra quills to sew a new shirt for her son."

The routine of winter camp continued; snows came and went. Sometimes the sun shone, sometimes it hid its face for days and the clouds scudded back and forth like leaves on a pond. The people were comfortable in their warm lodges or walking about in buffalo-skin moccasins with high tops, leggings of dark woolen cloth, red flannel geestrings and warm skin shirts with the hair inside. Children slid down the hills on buffalo-rib sleds, fished through the ice of the stream, played games. It was a good winter: *The Winter When Everything Was Good.*

Fox Dancer, wrapped in his blanket, watched Shell pulling Sun Hair in the snow on a piece of tanned hide. She was beautiful; cheeks glowed with health, her movements were graceful, the laugh sounded like a summer stream, tinkling its way over stones and rocks.

"Look!" she cried, pulling the laughing child up to him and panting for breath. Her teeth were white and even, her eyes sparkled; even her breath was sweet and clear like that of a child. "See how he laughs! He likes the snow!"

Fox Dancer touched a finger to the child's auburn curls, the color of forest leaves in autumn, tight-curled like Duffy's own. "He is happy. We are all happy. Rock and Thunder and Sun and Buffalo and the rest of the Great Ones have been good to us."

Good as the gods had been, he still bore a heavy responsibility. He knew he had aged in the last year. Not so much physical age, though there were new lines in his face, even a dusting of early gray in the locks Shell braided for him with wrappings of otter fur. Not so much an aging of the mind, either; he was alert and thoughtful as ever, pausing always to think things out, to decide whether this was the better course, or that. No, it was something else. It was a feeling of ancient sorrow, a feeling something was ending, some good and vital thing was withering, drying, brittling, dropping down into nothingness.

In The Moon When Raccoons Come Out winter still lay heavily on the Oglala land, but there were a few signs of spring. Weary of long inactivity, the whole camp looked forward to spring. Too, the Oglala allies, long in camp, were restless. There were fights between some of the Brulés and the Oglalas, between the visiting Crows and the Miniconjous. All of them longed for the taste of fresh green wild onion, a chance to ride from the winter-bound camp and stretch their legs, to eat plenty of fresh, fat meat, search for mushrooms, wild cabbage, cama roots.

Early one morning, waning moon low in the west and the

camp sleeping under a heavy crust of snow, the dogs started to bark. Instantly awake, Fox Dancer sat up in the buffalo robes.

"What is it?" Shell whispered from her bed across the fire.

He shook his head. "I do not know."

Again they listened. Sun Hair whimpered, then slept again. But as Fox Dancer lay down, the dogs repeated their chorus.

Naked, Fox Dancer went to stand at the tent flap. People called back and forth from lodge to lodge; the *tipis* glowed like giant candles as wood was thrown on dying fires. Lightning Man stood wrapped in his blanket outside the lodge. Had he been there all night, keeping watch? Fox Dancer wondered.

"What is it?" he asked.

Lightning Man shook his head. He had his rifle in the crook of his arm, and a belt of cartridges in one hand.

"I do not know," he muttered, "but I do not like this, what is happening."

Men were running from other lodges, pulling on shirts and leggings, fumbling at guns, waving lances. They were black shadows on the snow, hurrying this way and that.

Bent Nose, the Crow, pointed north. "That is where the noise is coming from," he announced.

Almost as he spoke there was a great commotion, a caterwauling of camp dogs. They scurried down into the camp from the heights, tails between legs, some looking back to bark, others whining and whimpering in fear.

Fox Dancer sprang up on a tree stump, shouting, "Come here! Listen to me! Go to your *tipis* and get all the ammunition you have! Tell the women and children to run into the woods! Then—then—"

He broke off, staring. Down the path from the northern entrance to the Oglala camp came a great black mass. Like a gigantic stain it moved, blotting out the snow in its spreading darkness. As it moved forward, he heard faint shouts, the neighing of horses, the brassy song of a cavalry bugle.

"Hurry!" Fox Dancer shouted. "Get ready! They are almost here!" He ran into the lodge and grabbed his rifle and all the ammunition he could find, cramming the pockets of his skin shirt with cartridges. "Go!" he screamed at Shell. "Take the baby and run, run to the trees!" Still holding the gun, he hopped awkwardly into his leggings, and fell, sprawled full-length. In panic his groping hand found a knife and a hatchet. He stuck those in his belt and ran outside.

The pony soldiers were so close he could see faces under their shaggy bearskin hats. They wallowed forward in the heavy snow, approaching faster than a man could run. The soldiers cheered, a wild shrill sound, and drawn sabers flashed.

"Run!" Fox Dancer shouted to Shell, and saw her hurry through the snow toward the forest, baby in her arms.

There was no chance to organize resistance. Like an avalanche from a mountain, the cavalry troopers rolled ponderously forward, sweeping everything in their path. Fox Dancer fired, and a soldier rolled from his horse and dropped into the snow like a great bear. The man lumbered to his feet and stood there, dazed, until Lightning Man drove his hatchet into the furry cap. "Devils!" old Bent Nose yelled, hurling his lance. "Devils! Devils! Devils!" Then a soldier rode him down, cleaving him from shoulder to breastbone with a whistling bloody saber.

The fight milled in and out of the *tipis*. Troopers with flaming brands ignited the dry skins and lodges flared up like torches. The night stank of burning grain, scorched meat, hides, furs; in one lodge a barrel of gunpowder ignited and the *tipi* sailed high into the air in a welter of broken poles and singed hides, falling down again to ignite other lodges.

At the lower end of the camp a detachment of cavalrymen tore down the brush corral. Whooping and yelling, they drove away the Oglala horses. Beside Fox Dancer, Scraper was singing his death song:

> "*Nothing lives long,*
> *Only the earth*
> *And the mountains!*"

Scraper did not live long, either. A trooper leaned down and pushed the muzzle of his carbine against Scraper's face, at the same time pulling the trigger. But in his death throe Scraper grabbed the man's booted leg, draggling him from the saddle. Fox Dancer had shot away all his ammunition. Now he picked up a lance and drove it through the soldier's body. "*Onhey!*" he shouted, wrenching the lance free. "I have overcome this one!"

Still the black stain spread, across the snow, past the burning lodges, even to the edge of the encircling forest. Among the trees there was commotion, the yelling of Hat People soldiers, screams of women. A half-grown boy dashed from behind a tree, floundering in snow, and rose again like a frightened animal, hands pressed over his ears against the shrieks and moans.

"Come away from here!" Lightning Man, hands bleeding, face blackened with smoke, pulled at Fox Dancer's arm. "There is nobody left to fight!"

Angry, Fox Dancer pushed away the hand. "It is all my fault! Look what has happened!" He shook his broken lance, howling at the gods in shame and frustration. "Rock, look at me! Thunder, Buffalo! Look at me! Look what I have done!"

Lightning Man hit him hard in the face. "I do not know what you have done," he panted, "but I know what we have to do now! It is a hard thing, but we have to to run away and fight them some other time!"

Streamers of red and yellow and gray lighted the eastern sky; clouds of smoke from the burning village rose into the air, then stopped to flatten out in a mushroom cloud that spread far distant. In the half-light the fight broke into small whorls of action. Bands of troopers surrounded smaller and smaller pockets of resistance, sometimes only a single Oglala, beleaguered and singing his death song.

"Come!" Lightning Man yelled, pulling his cousin away. "Come now! There is no time to think, the way you always do!"

Behind a screen of willows bordering the frozen river they escaped into the forest. As they hurried into its blackness they saw broken bodies in the undergrowth, shot and slashed where they had hidden. A small girl threw her arms around her dead mother; when she saw them, she called, "Help me, brothers! My mother is hurt!"

When Fox Dancer paused, Lightning Man shoved him roughly ahead. "There is no time for anything," he growled. "The woman is dead, and the girl will have to eat roots!"

↔

For three days they stayed in the mountains with about a hundred of the people who had escaped the carnage. There were a handful of Miniconjous, too, and Brulés; a half-dozen Crows. They managed to catch a few of their scattered horses and now they sat them high on the side of the mountain, watching the pony soldiers return to Fort Jackson across the snow plains. What remained of their winter supplies had been packed on the Oglalas' own horses by the cavalrymen. There was no real reason now to return to the ruined camp.

"There are not many of us anymore," a Crow said. His mangled ear still bled, and he had a dirty rag wrapped around it.

The winter camp had been a great gathering, bigger and richer than any in the time of Blue Horse or Elk River. Now the survivors were only a handful, hungry, low on ammunition, defeated, and discouraged. The power of the Sioux no longer lay across the road of the fire wagons.

"There are enough of us," Fox Dancer murmured.

They all looked at him. "Enough? Enough for what?"

He gestured. "I will tell you later. But those white men will be sorry they did not hunt us down and kill us all."

No one really wanted to go but they rode into the camp for a final look, a farewell to family and old friends, goodbye to memories of a last happy winter. In single file they rode, silent, each man scarred from wounds, splashed with dried blood, their clothing torn and stained.

The Oglala winter camp was a shambles. Lodges, food, blankets; all smoldered and stank. Where the burning lodges had collapsed there were now black holes in the snow. A stray pony, bleeding from a gunshot wound, watched them with listless eyes; dead bodies, scattered like broken, castoff dolls, were beginning to bloat and smell. In the remains of Fox Dancer's lodge he found the twisted remains of the Hat People's three-legged god, glass broken, brass melted. Its legs were burned into ashen ghosts that vanished at his touch. The Hat People's god had made him a great man. Finally it had betrayed him.

They saw him squatting before the remains of the transit, and Little Man said, "You do not need that thing anyway, brother." Someone else said, "Fox Dancer was born a chief. He does not need a Hat People god. He has his own medicine."

Sun shone brightly on the carnage. Man-Who-Never-Walked was dead, crumpled over an old musket outside his *tipi,* where he had dragged himself to fight. Twin Woman was dead, too, in the blackened ruins of the lodge. Bull Head, Limber Lance, Yellow Lodge, Differently Colored, Cut Finger, Bent Nose, Woman's Heart—so many dead! Fox Dancer put his hands over his face, trying to blot out the scene. Even then he could see desolation, ruin, the end of a way of life.

"What are you thinking, cousin?" Lightning Man asked. His face was smeared with blood and soot, his eyes red-rimmed.

Fox Dancer kept his hands in front of his face. He was remembering his young man's dream, the dream of the dancing foxes. *First they welcomed him in and bade him try the steps of their intricate dance.*

Goosey said something to Lightning Man in a low voice. Fox Dancer's cousin walked to the edge of the woods. There, half hidden behind a winter-killed bush, lay Shell and her baby. Sun Hair's small body had been almost cut in two by a saber slash. Shell had tried vainly to defend the child; she lay across it protectively, dead from bullet holes in the back of her shell-decorated shirt.

Lightning Man dropped to his knees. He pulled Shell away from her child, cradling her in his arms. Goosey respectfully averted his face and went back to rummaging in the debris of his one-time *tipi,* salvaging what he could. His woman was dead, too.

Lightning Man loved her, Fox Dancer thought. He never said it, no more than I did, but my cousin loved Shell too. Shell died for Duffy, for Sun Hair, for Lightning Man, for him, too.

Finally, as they all watched, Lightning Man gently laid Shell down. Finding a blood-spattered blanket nearby, he spread it over mother and child, piling stones on the bodies to keep animals away.

"*Hopo!*" Fox Dancer said. "It is time to go away from here."

As they rode off, a shabby and battleworn file, Fox Dancer again thought of the foxes and their midnight dance. In his dream the principal fox, the chief of foxes, became angry at the interloper. He thought the young Oglala had discovered their secret. Now he saw the fox face again, features sharp and clear in a window of his mind. The principal fox had been Lew Duffy. Fox Dancer discovered the secret of the foxes, and The People had been destroyed because of it.

# CHAPTER THIRTEEN

All that spring Fox Dancer's ragged band stayed near Fort Andrew Jackson; not near enough to be discovered, but near enough to watch from the high bluff where they once tied Lew Duffy when they rode in high spirits to the post to bargain for the Irishman's ransom.

Now soldiers came and went. Supply wagons toiled in from the East, unloaded, went back empty. Each morning a striped flag went up the pole, and they heard distant strains of a bugle, playing the get-up song. Many of the Oglalas were sad and discouraged; some were sick, all were hungry. Some nights one or two slipped away. There remained only a hard core of about fifty, bound together by Fox Dancer's vow to punish Lew Duffy, architect of their misfortunes.

Day after day, night after night, they maintained the watch. Game lurked in the rolling hills, but the Oglalas had little ammunition, saving it against the day they would reckon with the red-hair man. Besides, they did not want to make any noise. A few had bows, sometimes killing rabbits and small deer, but the meat did not go far. Fox Dancer was thin and hollow-eyed; he insisted everyone else eat first, and he took whatever was left. Something nourished the burning in him; the Oglalas thought it was his hate for Duffy. Even Lightning Man was afraid of his gaunt cousin.

"Duffy will come out sometime!" Fox Dancer insisted. "It is spring! The buds are sticking out on the willows, and birds are making nests. Duffy will come out! A man like him cannot stay long in a narrow box like that fort!"

Wood parties did emerge occasionally, scouring the hills.

Though winter had passed they still needed wood for the cook-
stoves of the pony-soldier messes. The Oglalas skirted the routes
of the wood parties, and the soldiers ranged farther and farther
afield as they searched the denuded hills. Their foes moved
quietly, like shadows, careful to stay downwind. A cavalry horse
could smell Indians, and so give an alarm.

The wood parties usually included only a few privates, a sergeant, a team, and wagon. Frustrated, Fox Dancer sent some of
his people to ride a circuitous route to the grasslands east of the
fort, where Lew Duffy might be traveling in the lightly escorted
wagon trains that plied the rutted trail to the railhead. But no
one saw Duffy; the Irishman seemed a ghost, a *sikisn*. Some,
who had never seen Duffy or who had forgotten him, began
to wonder if the red-hair man truly existed.

The Oglalas got help from the *wagluhke*, the "hang-around-
the-fort people" they despised. The *wagluhke* were frightened
of the fierce Oglalas, and readily promised to keep watch for
Lew Duffy. One later reported that he had seen the red-hair
man taking the air, strolling about the parapet on fine days.
But that was all.

Finally the Oglalas became mutinous. Only a few, like Lightning Man and Fox Dancer, wanted to stay on in the fruitless
hunt. Many had friends and relatives in other bands, other
tribes. They were all weary from hunger and lack of sleep. But
Fox Dancer shamed them with his scorn.

"You are not men!" he shouted. "You are rabbits! Do you
remember what happened back there? Do you remember the
way the Hat People sneaked up on us that night and killed so
many? Do you remember how women and children died?" Turning pale with rage, he shook a fist. "You are cowards!" He
made a contemptuous sign; fists before him, index fingers poked
stiffly out, then drawing his hands quickly back and down,
curving the thin fingers like claws. *You cannot stand before
me; you shrink away!*

They did indeed shrink away, uneasy at his wild eyes, sunken
cheeks. Most agreed to stay a few days longer. But there was

muttering, shaking of heads. "He is crazy! Fox Dancer is crazy!" they said.

One fine day in The Moon When Strawberries Ripen a *wagluhke* ran all the way from the post to tell them the news.

"The red-hair man is coming!"

Excited, they crowded around. Fox Dancer clamped the man's arm in his fingers and demanded, "How do you know?"

Panting for breath, the *wagluhke* said, "We saw him! Right now he is going around the fort, getting soldiers to come with him to look for wood. There is a big wagon—no, two wagons— and teams of horses. The red-hair man sat in the wagon. He was playing a kind of music thing with strings to it—strings he picked at with a piece of shell. A banjo, it is called."

The Oglalas ran to the sparse stand of cottonwoods over-looking the valley. The *wagluhke* was right, at least about the wagons. Two of them, each drawn by a double span of big horses, were starting up the slope toward the hill where the Oglalas camped. A mounted column accompanied the wagons, perhaps thirty yellowlegs. Was Duffy really with them?

"I saw him!" the *wagluhke* insisted. "He was sitting right in the wagon! I do not tell lies!"

The party was a big one, perhaps enlarged for a lengthy expedition. Fox Dancer watched the distant wagons for a long time. Then he said to Goosey, "Keep your eye on this man! If he has told me lies, I will cut off his privates and feed them to the magpies!" Quickly he gave orders to the rest. "Pick up every-thing—all bones and scraps, everything, and bury them. Bury night-soil, put out the fire and spread the ashes wide. Cover the ashes with grass and dirt. If the wagons pass this way, they will not know anyone has been here!"

Excited at the prospect of action after weeks of lying in wait, the Oglalas quickly ran about, disposing of everything that might betray their presence. Men checked cartridges, ran thumbs along the keen edges of lances, made sure tasseled knives were free in scabbards, ready to draw and strike. Hatchets were honed on rocks, horses given a last watering, belts tightened, and sagging eagle feathers adjusted upright.

"We are going to kill all those pony soldiers," Fox Dancer told them, voice trembling with excitement. "I promise you that, as I promise to all our friends who died when the yellow-legs attacked our camp! We are going to go very careful, like the fox, not putting a paw down till he knows where the next paw will go. We will stay a little way ahead, keep out of sight. But watch always where they are going! And no man is to shoot a gun or anything unless I tell him. Nobody—" He looked fiercely around, feathered lance clenched in his fist. "Nobody hurt the red-hair man! When the time for fighting comes, the red-hair man must be brought to me! I will take care of him!"

Silent and unseen, they drifted ahead of the crawling wagons, using every trick and stratagem to stay concealed. That night the troopers camped in a willow-choked draw near a stream. Where the Oglalas squatted, silent in the night and chewing scanty bits of old meat, they could smell the campfire of the soldiers, hear shouting and laughter and jokes, the plinking of a banjo. Some wanted to attack right then, pouring into the draw and killing the soldiers where they slept. But Fox Dancer disagreed.

"They are too near the fort, and might get help. As long as they keep riding to the west, we stay near them and watch."

Someone objected. "We have all been away a long time! Let us do it now, get it over, and go our ways!" But when Fox Dancer glowered, the man shrugged and walked away.

Next morning, under a cloudless sky, the Army wagons rolled westward again. The Oglalas, skirting the progress of the wood party, saw they were apparently heading for a cleft in the hills. Scouts sent by Fox Dancer found a large stand of pine and oak trees in the cleft. A spring of good water poured from the hillside, and below was a grassy bottom with rich forage. The cleft must be the white men's destination.

Late in the afternoon the Oglalas reached the cleft and rode along the slopes, careful to leave no sign. Meadow larks sang, the chirping of thousands of grasshoppers made a steady din. Far overhead an eagle soared, looking down at them. Go *away*,

*Brother Eagle!* Fox Dancer prayed. *The white men will see you, be warned!*

The bird pumped its wings and soared toward the setting sun. Carefully the Oglalas chose their ambush. Not too near the spring, that was dangerous. Not in the bottoms, where the wise old cavalry mounts might scent them. Instead, they tied their horses high on an uncomfortable ledge commanding a view of the valley below, downwind, again, from the place where the yellowlegs would camp.

At dusk Lightning Man squatted beside his cousin on the rocky ledge. Though it was late spring the air was cold. They wrapped themselves in blankets, watching the wagon train top the rise, rumble down the slopes toward water, the rich grass. Even from that distance they heard the squeak and jingle of harness, a sergeant calling to an outrider. Goosey, long deprived of a smoke, claimed he could smell pipe tobacco. The yellow winks of lanterns came on, the wagons stopped beside the rocky pool below the spring. Men sprang down to light fires, fry meat, boil coffee.

"When do we hit them?" Lightning Man whispered.

Fox Dancer pointed to the yellow moon just showing its face over the rolling hills. "When Moon is at the top of that tree, then will be the time."

It was a long way for the moon to go, and some were impatient. But Lightning Man agreed with his cousin, saying, "They will be asleep then! They will all be asleep, like our people when the pony soldiers came in fur coats to kill us that time."

The moon climbed higher, became pale and small. Nightbirds called, an owl drifted on silent wings. From a far peak a coyote yipped, a small shower of music. Together the Oglalas watched the ascent of the silver disk.

"Now?" Lightning Man asked.

Fox Dancer took a deep breath. "Soon!"

In a few minutes he rose, walking among his men. He made them check cartridges, chamber fresh loads; there would be no other chance. Carefully he gave them instructions. One party,

under Lightning Man, would sweep straight down into the
camp; another, under Little Man, would gallop along the edge
of the valley, flanking the camp, then turn back to strike it
from the other side. Fox Dancer himself would take Goosey,
the frightened *wagluhke,* and a few others to throw strength
wherever it was needed.

"Our dead people," he told them, "are there in the Camp
in the Sky, watching. All men be brave. Do not disgrace those
who died in the winter camp." He held up a warning finger.
"Remember—no one is to hurt the red-hair man! Bring him
to me."

He took a final look at the sleeping camp of the yellowlegs.
Campfires burned low, no voices were heard. The rising moon
shed patches of silver on wagons, grass, the tethered horses.
Then he yelled, "*Hopo!* Let's go!"

Suddenly, excitingly, it was the reverse of what had happened in the Oglala winter camp. The Sioux broke over the
pony-soldier camp like flood water over a beaver dam, foaming,
churning, carrying everything before them. Frightened yellow-
legs milled this way and that, searching for weapons. One, in
his panic, dragged the issue blanket he had lately slept in. Some
of the soldiers had slept in the empty wagons, and the Oglalas
lanced and chopped them in the way they speared trapped fish
in a weir. There were screams and yells, flashes of guns in the
night, smells of powder and blood and fear. Behind one of the
wagons a group of skilled veterans rallied under the leadership
of an officer—it was Lew Duffy—starting a withering counterfire.
But Little Man's warriors, having flanked the camp, galloped
in from the other side and caught the defenders on their blind
side.

One of the soldiers started in panic to run and blundered into
Goosey, who had dismounted and was hacking with his hatchet
at whatever white flesh or blue cloth ornamented with yellow
piping he could find. "*Onhey!*" he kept shouting. "*Onhey!*"
In the smoky moonlight he ran after the fleeing cavalryman.
On reaching him, hatchet upraised, Goosey was astonished to

see the soldier suddenly turn, put the muzzle of the pistol in his own mouth, and pull the trigger.

Elsewhere the battle swirled and boiled, but there could only be one outcome. There had been thirty or so of the soldiers; now the rich grass was littered with crumpled blue. Six or eight of the defenders still pressed around Lew Duffy, with the wagon at their back. But the wagon was on fire, and that shelter could not last long. Flames and smoke billowed into the sky. As Fox Dancer signaled his own small contingent into the fight, he saw Lightning Man climb into the burning wagon from the far side and shoot down at the defenders. One man fell, then another. A third looked up with desperate white face, and Lightning Man cut the face in two with his hatchet.

"*Onhey!*" he shouted. "That is for Man-Who-Never-Walked and his woman!"

Duffy's saber slashed and sparkled in the fire-streaked night. The Irishman had lost his hat, his shirt was almost torn off, blood and soot stained his chest. Now he was alone, utterly alone, but the fox still had a sharp bite. One of the Oglalas ventured close to the whirling saber; the shining blade caught him in the side with a dull, chunking sound. Suddenly the flesh opened up, liver and guts and shiny things spilled out.

"Don't kill Duffy!" Fox Dancer screamed, trying to push his way through the attackers. "Don't kill him!"

Thrusting, slashing, parrying the lances that menaced him, the Irishman screamed imprecations. "Red bastards! Come and get me, then!" He lunged at Little Man, but at that moment Fox Dancer's cousin flung himself from the wagon above and wrapped his arms around Duffy. He and the red-hair man fell heavily to the ground, the blade of the saber caught in a rocky ledge and broke with a metallic clink. Lightning Man's fingers were around Duffy's throat, and suddenly everything was quiet. The moon floated high in the sky, ragged streamers of smoke from the burning wagons drifted across the night, somewhere a nightbird sang, awakened by tumult.

"Don't kill him!" Fox Dancer repeated. He knelt beside the two men, intertwined among the rocks. Others helped him, pried away Lightning Man's fingers from Duffy's throat. "I told you, cousin! He is for me!"

Even then, some of them had to pull Lightning Man back. Panting and fierce, he tried to get at the Irishman. They had to grab his arms hard and hold him.

"I broke your goddamned fingers once, didn't I?" Duffy said. "Ah, you bastard!" In his hand he still held the handle of the broken saber. Shrugging, he tossed the handle away, saying through split and broken lips, "Ah, you're all bastards! Red bastards, too, and that's a very special kind. Even dogs are better than red bastards!"

One of the cavalrymen had only been dazed by a blow on the head. From the corner of his eye Fox Dancer saw the man raise his head, listen, then start to drag himself on his elbows through the tall grass. Fox Dancer gestured, and Little Man pierced the soldier with his lance as casually as he might spear a trout. For a moment they watched the man, pinned to the ground, wriggle the same way a fish does. Then his movements grew less violent, and finally he was still, life spilled from him into the grasses and rocks. Little Man put a moccasined foot on the blue back, yanking free the blade of the lance. He looked disgusted; there was no glory in counting coup like that.

"It has been a long time," Fox Dancer said. Leaning on his pennoned lance, he looked at Lew Duffy. "And a long way, too! I did not see you since we were in Washington, together, there at the Great Council House of the Hat People."

Duffy licked his lips, still rubbing his throat. Once he had broken Lightning Man's fingers, but they were still very powerful.

"Yes," he croaked. "It *has* been a long time! Sweet Jesus, everything has been a long time, hasn't it? It seems like a long time ago, everything I ever did."

Fox Dancer nodded his head toward the cleft through which the wagons had come. "We did not see you at our winter camp, when the yellowlegs attacked us in the night, in the snow, killed all our people—women, children, old men, one even who could not walk, and his old woman, too."

The Irishman's voice was hoarse and trembling, but there was no fear in him. "I begged off," he said. "The general said all right, you don't have to go, you've done the Sioux enough damage. You see, the idea for the winter campaign was mine. I'd thought about it for a long time, ever since you held me prisoner that time."

They were silent, ringing about him while the woodwork of the wagons crackled and smoked. Then Lightning Man, fondling his once-broken fingers, snarled, "What is all this talk for? Cousin, why do we not kill him now, take the food and things from the wagons before they burn up, get away from here right now?"

"Sweet Jesus, yes!" Duffy said. "Kill me and have done with it! What more's to be said?"

Duffy was a brave man; they liked that in him. But Duffy was the fox, too. His auburn locks shone in the flames, moustache curled luxuriantly rich and red.

"Kill me!" Duffy insisted. With a quick gesture he tore aside the remnants of his shirt, exposing the matted pelt of his chest, red and glossy against the pale skin. "Goddamnit, what are you waiting for!" He gestured toward Fox Dancer's feathered lance. "Take that goddamned pigsticker and run it right through here!" He pointed. "Make an end to it, now! Hurry!"

When no one moved, the Irishman went on talking, almost as if to himself. "There's no question about the guilt! There's not even grounds for appeal, is there? By God, I did it, and I'm not about to crawl on my ass for mercy, even if Sioux bastards knew anything about the tender feeling, which same I doubt." He wiped a hand across his lips, staring at Fox Dancer. "I sold you out in Washington, you know that. Well, I did!" He lifted his head defiantly. "And do you know what?" He clutched at his shoulder, ripped off the ornament holding it out for all to see. "Old Dan Cardwell never even gave me the silver eagles he promised! It was lies, all lies, a way to get Duffy to pull their damned chestnuts out of the fire!" He threw down the silver bars, and they were lost in the high grass. "It'll go down in the *Army and Navy Journal*," he said bitterly. "Duffy, Lewis. Captain!" He howled the word. "Captain!" It echoed down the valley, carroming from rocky ledge to ledge till it was lost in the night. "After fifteen years of better soldiering than any of the fat-ass coffee-coolers back at the Department!" He broke down, sobbing, and put his face in his hands.

This was the time to kill him. Duffy knew what he had done, they knew what he had done, no more was to be extracted from the scene. *Kill him now, stop all this talking, take the food and things from the wagons and go, go now.* By the time the sun came up the Oglalas must be a long way from this place. But as Fox Dancer raised his lance and stepped forward, a terrible feeling came over him, a sensation of light-headedness, almost fear.

For a moment he paused, still balancing the lance. The Irishman did not raise his head, only waited, hands over his face, weeping.

"What is the matter?" Lightning Man demanded. "Hurry, cousin! It is time!"

Again Fox Dancer raised his lance. Again the strange feeling spread through him. He stared at the glossy red hair, the curling moustache, the mat of hair on the chest, bright as fox's brush after a long summer when it is fat and sleek, filled with plump rabbits and unwary quail.

"Kill him!" Lightning Man shouted. "What are you waiting for?"

*Duffy was a fox, and he was the Fox Dancer.* A bond, a nameless cord, bound them together. Speechless, trembling, Fox Dancer raised the lance, sighting along the blade at the chest hair. Duffy was the chief of the foxes, and he the Fox Dancer.

"Well?" Duffy peered through his fingers. "Hail Mary, Hail Mary, Hail Mary! Hail Mary! I forget the rest of it, but get it the hell over with!" His voice started to plead, then rose to a scream. "Kill me! Kill me! Kill me!"

Fox Dancer raised the lance high. They all saw the shining blade shake with the strange passion that gripped him. "Strike!" Little Man howled.

But he did not strike. Instead, he drove the lance half its

length into the ground. For a moment the handle vibrated, then was still.

Duffy stared in amazement. They all looked on, mouths open. What was happening? Then they realized that Fox Dancer was in the grip of a great confrontation with his own medicine. No one spoke.

Fox Dancer stood for a long time, staring at the lance. Then he stepped forward and put his foot against it, breaking off the handle where it entered the ground. Without a word he raised the splintered stick and brought it down on Duffy. Silently, furiously, he beat the red-hair man with the handle, raining blows on the Irishman's head and face, shoulders, and arms. Duffy bled, the white skin showed welts, a flailing blow crushed some teeth. But the Irishman did not flinch. He kept his head upright until Fox Dancer, exhausted by passion and force of blows, tossed the stick away and rushed into the darkness.

For a long time he stood behind the wagon, thinking. No one approached. He only half heard the commotion back in the firelight. The Oglalas were rummaging through the wagons, catching scattered cavalry horses, lashing supplies into bundles—sacks of corn, the bacon they loved, coffee, powder and ball, paper cartridges, too. They would not be hungry for a long time.

Fox Dancer was still standing there, thinking, when Lightning Man came up to him. He did not any longer need the Hat People's three-legged god to see truth, see far into the future. In his mind's eye he could see the fire wagons coming, despoiling the land with their smoke and steam, spinning an iron web, trapping and destroying The People. Plainly and clearly he saw the truth, what was coming. Perhaps The People could not stop it, but as men they would fight against it to the inevitable end.

"It is time to go, cousin," Lightning Man said.

"Yes. I know."

Lightning Man put something in his hand. It was warm, and soft, and stickily wet. In the light of the moon, the fires from the burning wagons, it was easy to see what it was. It was the hair of the fox—Lew Duffy's red hair.

"Tell everybody to get ready," Fox Dancer said. "We have a long way to go."

Sitting on his pony, he looked up at the Broken Back Star. Up there, to the north somewhere, were brave men who would help him fight the Hat People. Brave young men like Gall, Sitting Bull, Crazy Horse. There were a lot of the Hat People, but there were many Sioux, too—and it was their country.

# BIBLIOGRAPHY

*Warpath* by Stanley Vestal, Houghton-Mifflin Co., Boston, Mass., 1934

*Red Men Calling on the Great White Father* by Katharine C. Turner, University of Oklahoma Press, Norman, Okla., 1951

*Life and Adventures of Frank Grouard* by Joe DeBarthe, University of Oklahoma Press, Norman, Okla., 1958

*On the Border With Crook* by John G. Bourke, Charles Scribner's Son, New York, N.Y., 1891

*The Indian Sign Language* by W. P. Clark, L. R. Hamersly & Co., Philadelphia, Pa., 1885

*Reveille in Washington* by Margaret Leech, Harper & Brothers, New York, N.Y., 1941

*Touch the Earth* by T. C. McLuhan, Outerbridge & Dienstfrey, New York, N.Y., 1971

*The Look of the Old West* by Foster Harris, Viking Press, New York, N.Y., 1955

*The Soldiers* by David Nevin, Time-Life Books, New York, N.Y., 1973

*The Indian and the Horse* by Frank Gilbert Roe, University of Oklahoma Press, Norman, Okla., 1955